Fraternity

U. V. ERNEST

DENVER, COLORADO

For my Dad and Mum,
Much love.

Acknowledgment

I appreciate the members of all fraternities, especially those who live up to the good ideals, goals or objectives of whatever fraternity they have chosen to affiliate themselves with.

Let it also be known that my appreciation is deep to all those friends of mine in the various fraternities who also enlightened me about what their fraternity stood for.

Of course it goes without saying that God is deeply, with my whole being appreciated. Words are not even enough to express my gratitude. He saw me through thick and thin.

Any fraternity is as good as another
so long as the fraternity's underlying principle
is to be their brothers keeper in and out.
~ Author

PROLOGUE

IN THE EARLY days in Nigeria, higher education was almost an exclusive right of children from wealthy homes. As a result, it led to differences in social class previledge.

For those who were not from wealthy homes, they had no option but to take seriously their education so as to merit the prize of an academic degree but many others had to feel the life of youth and so took advantage of the environment they found themselves to join the aristocrats who were flashier and more connected. They became so good that some even manage to outshine the natural elite.

Not surprisingly, as it is with humanity from the beginning of time, there begin to arise different students' clubs; all trying to be more superior to the other.

It was also around this era in the 1950s that tribalism became so rampant in the country which also affected the students. The University College, Ibadan, the first ackwoledged higher institution in the country bacame so affected with the disease of tribalism that all forms of students activities bacame biased.

That being the case, seven students came together to form

the PYRATES CONFRATERNITY (PC) in 1952 to combat these negative tendencies with their original scroll written and signed by the founding fathers: Wole Soyinka, Ralph Okpara, Pious Oleghe, Ikpehare Imoukhuede, Nathaniel Oyeola, Olumuyiwa Awe and Sylvanus U. Eghuche. Known as the original seven, their names remain a most valued item in the Pyrates treasure chest

Chapter 1

Professor Muyiwa, a handsome, slim, dark complexioned, middle aged man had an eye like that of a snake, so small but alert, a mouth of tiny lips, a small nose and a face like it has been carved out of stone, was a husband who doesn't like to be hungry. He claims that the slightest sign of hunger can make him dizzy. And once dizzy, he cannot concentrate on what he is doing. And so on many occasions, he told his wife to make sure there's something to eat. He made sure he gives her extra spending money. His wife, knowing the kind of man she married, made it her duty to make sure the family had something to eat even between meals.

But on this fateful day maybe because she was tired of the routine of her daily chores or because there was no serious rapport between them as before, she delayed his breakfast. When it was time for him to leave, she asked: Do you want breakfast?

"What are my choices?" the husband asked.

"Yes or No?" she asked again. The husband, noticing the tone with which she asked knew better than to fight it. He knew that these past few weeks, he hadn't been much of a husband to her. He simply said,"whatever." Although he had the kind of face that would frighten a little baby, nonetheless he was benign inside especially with his wife. The only place he was firm was when it came to educational standard. This was the area he doesn't compromise his stand and it was the area that was giving him problem with students. He couldn't understand why a student who didn't come for his lectures expected to pass his papers. Some few weeks earlier, he had received a threat note from an anonymous student who claimed he had written the professor's course two times now and failed and the next will be the 3rd time. The anonymous student made it clear in the note that the professor's wife will be a widow should the professor fail him the 3rd time. This was in the late 1960's. Although the professor had been hearing false rumours of how fellow lecturers like himself have been receiving threat notes, he never thought it would get to his turn. Worse was that the threat had included murder. The others he had been hearing never included murder. He had heard of breaking of windshields, flattening of car tires, even lighting up offices but none had included murder. What made a chill ran dawn his spine was the mention of his wife becoming a widow.

For the 20 years of their marriage, they have really enjoyed each other. The thought of his wife alone or even re-marrying was something he could not bear. What was he to do? He kept asking himself. He had been a lecturer long enough to know that everybody cannot pass an exam. Some will pass and some will fail, if only he can fish out the student. He has tried a number of times by asking if there was anybody who had failed his course two times. But it seems most of the students were writing his course for the first time. Another thing again was even if he granted leniency to a large percentage of the students writing his course, will the particular student be among them or should he leave the school for another? How was he going to explain that to his wife? These were the thoughts bothering him and the reason he had been distant from his wife.

The wife had already prepared his breakfast of 2 slices of toast bread and a cup of coffee. When she called him to the table, she had asked him if she should open a can of sardine but he had said 'no'. The wife for the past 20 years had still not been able to figure him out. How can a man who complains he is dizzy at the slightest sign of hunger not eat much? She had told her friend and her friend had said "there's a part of every human that is ironical." She stored it at the back of her mind. After eating his breakfast, he picked up his bag kissed his wife goodbye. The wife on the other hand couldn't help but wonder what was wrong with her husband. She had noticed that in the past few weeks, something had been eating him up. She had asked one time and he had said, "nothing."

Over the years they've always shared their problems and more often then not, a solution was always just around the corner. One of her greatest assets was patience; so she told herself to wait.

On entering the class, prof. Muyiwa greeted the students: "Hello students!" the class replied: "Good morning Sir."

"Today we are going to be treating…." before he could finish the statement, a student walked into the class. Prof. Muyiwa paused. He looked at the student. Prof. Muyiwa as a person had zero tolerance for indiscipline of any kind. He had a strict injunction about entering his class after he had stepped into the class. But because of the death threat he had received, he decided to be lenient with the students. So instead of walking the student out of his class as usual he asked "Why are you just coming?" hoping that with a good explanation, he'll pardon him. The student said:"Sir, I was walking with a girl."

"It is either you give me a justifiable answer or you walk out of my class." The Prof. said.

"Sir, she was walking very slowly." The class burst into laughter. The professor was sad for him. Not because he had came late to his class but because his parents, who were top politicians in the country were too busy finding ways to steal money from the government had failed to impart in him the discipline needed as a man to be strong especially in the rainy days. Prof. Muyiwa wasn't really mad when he said "Just leave the class." He was hoping with the leniency he is showing, the student who had issued him a note of death threat might change his mind if really he planned anything of such. It was after the incident that he realized that the students had been misinterpreting his kindness for weakness. The incident taught him a lesson that it is better to be feared than to be loved as a man. 45 minutes later, he ended his class.

Three weeks later exams started. He made his questions easy so that a large percentage of his class can pass his course. Still it happened that some people failed. The next few weeks, he tried to be more observant, watching out for anybody who might be stalking him but he didn't notice anybody. Then he relaxed. He became close to his wife again. The wife, noticing the change became happy too. What the hell, their love life grew stronger again, especially in the night. Although their kids were in boarding schools, but because of work they had to spend most of the day outside. But at night, they tried to make good use of it. Sometimes in the night before easing off to sleep he would ask God the question again: "O Lord, what acts of thanksgiving shall I render you?" You have blessed me with a good wife, beautiful children and other good things of life. Where do I start from in thanking you? He was a faithful Catholic who brought up his children in the fear of God. As far as he was concerned, *life is beautiful.*

The following weekend happened to be the mid-term break for his kids in the boarding school. They came home happy. Their mother was so excited to see them but she noticed with a little sadness that they are underfed but then in the few days they would be spending at home, she would make sure there's enough to eat so that they can add some weight before going back to school.

The Sunday before the day they were supposed to go back to school, Prof. Muyiwa decided to take the family out for a picnic. Their mother had already cooked a great meal which they will eat there. On the way, Prof. bought some Coca-cola drinks to rinse the mouth. They were only five in the family: The father, mother, two boys and a girl. There was a fine garden in the government residential area (GRA). The man parked along the road and they all went into the garden. After like 30 minutes when they were fully relaxed, the mother asked her last child who was a boy of five "Junior, what did you learn in Sunday school today?"

"Well, mum, our teacher told us how God sent Moses behind enemy line on a rescue mission to lead the Israelites out of Egypt. When he got to the Red Sea, he had his engineers built a pontoon bridge and all the people walked across safely. Then he used his walkie talkie to radio headquarters for reinforcement. They sent bombers to blow up the bridge and saved the Israelites."

The mum was worried so she asked, "Now Junior, is that really what your teacher taught you?"

"Well, no mom, but if I tell it the way the teacher said it, you'd never believe it. He thinks we are still kids he can just lie to. He doesn't know we are grown ups."

The father laughed and laughed then he asked him "So you are a grown up guy, huh?"

"Well, not like you dad, but old enough to tell the difference between fiction and fact". The whole family laughed and laughed. It was really a good day. 30 minutes later they were through with their picnic. The next day the children left for school. After Prof. had dropped them off, it was still early enough to go of his office in school. He had just finished marking his scripts. What was left was to submit the result to the department and post it on the department's notice board. It took him 30 minutes to take care of that. By the time he got home, it was some few minutes after 12:00hrs. The wife had gone to work. She will not be back until 14:00hrs. He decided to do some reading before she comes. The following day happened to be a meeting for the entire lecturers in the department. That morning before leaving he said to the wife after breakfast: "What shall I get you when coming back?" he had had a great night in rear of the morning and so he was excited. The wife said "Just come back in one piece and that would be more than a present for me." She was an old fashioned woman who doesn't believe in extravagancy or spending money on things irrelevant.

"You know, there are a million reasons why I love you, if only I can count them for you."

"Don't worry, this night we'll see about that."

"Honey, you are the best." The husband replied then he kissed her goodbye and left for the meeting.

Coming back, he wanted to impress his wife with some thing she'll appreciate. He drove to a plaza close to the university to look for something that was not too expensive and not too cheap as well. Finding it, he quickly settled the bill and left. He wanted to get home as quickly as he could. It was 18:40hrs already. The meeting had drained his energy. He just wanted to get home and rest. By the time he got home it was 19:05 hrs and a little darker than as before. He was about to hoot the horn for the gatekeeper to open the gate when he saw four boys in black and black in faceless masks rushed out from the street beside his house.

Instinct told him they were coming for him but before he could put the gear into reverse, one of the boys had switched off the ignition and collected the key. Almost simultaneously, the door of the driver's seat was flung open. He was dragged out forcibly to the ground. Then they started beating him. The people in the streets thinking they are armed rubbers fled for safety. After like 20minutes of beating, kicking and stabbing, Prof became unconscious. Just when it was obvious he was dead, they left leaving the bloodstained body on the ground. After about 10minutes later when he regained consciousness, he began asking for help with a voice he thought was some-body else's. It was barely audible that he had to strain himself to hear his own voice. Although the gatekeeper knew the Prof. is around but for fear of the big guys beating him mercilessly when he peeped through a hole in the gate, knew better than to interfere. It was almost 35minutes later he peeped again to discover the hoodlums had gone and his boss was on the ground asking for help. He quickly went inside the house to call his boss' wife who was busy in the kitchen preparing what they'll eat that night. *"Madam, oga dey outside o, bad people don beat am O. I beg come make we go help am o, he dey ask…"* But the wife would not wait anymore to hear him. She quickly rushed out of the house to the gate. When she opened the gate and saw her husband lying there on the ground with so much blood over him, she started crying. She screamed for help which made other neighbors to come out. The key of the man's gray Peugeot 505 was on the floor of the car. A neighour quickly started the car and rushed him to a nearby hospital.

—•((•))•—

"Ahoy me seadoy"

"Ahoy me rugged brother".

The former Bamidele and the latter Christopher. Bamidele continued;

"Did you hear what happened last night?"

"Rumour has it that Prof. Muyiwa was beaten to death in front of his house." Christopher answered.

"I was told he was rushed to the hospital maybe he would survive it." Bamidele said. "The chances are slim though." Christopher said. "I am going to miss him. He is such a kind hearted man despite that he is strict." Bamidele said.

"Yes that is true. There's no way you can fail his course unless you do not come for his lectures." Christopher said.

"Yes! I had an A in his course last semester" Bamidele said. "Me too." said Christopher

"Ahoy do you think the pyrates are behind this HIT?" Bamidele asked

"I don't know, I have been hearing rumours, some people tend to think that we are responsible for the threat note being issued to lecturers these days. What do you think?"

Bamidele thought for a moment then said; "this is not going to be good if it is true. When I was inducted into this fraternity the orientation I was given was that this is a noble confraternity that do not involve herself in violent acts. That more than anything else, they must stand up for the weak and oppressed in the society. Especially students maltreated or denied their rights by the school authority. What do you think the steerer (captain of the pyrate ship at deck levels) is going to do if it is true?" Christopher asked.

That reminds me, there's a signal for a meeting at 18:00hrs tomorrow. The A.P will be at Honey Comb motels. I guess we'll find out what really happened and who was behind it. I have no doubt of what will happen to the person if he is a dog." Bamidele answered then looked at his watch which was reading 11:03hrs. He said, "hey dog, I have got a class by 11:15hrs. I guess I should start floating. Sail away dog"

<hr />

"Sail away me rugged brother" Christopher replied.

"Doctor, is my husband going to be ok?" The doctor, some few steps out of the operating room was confronted by Mrs. Muyiwa.

"Yes Madam, he is going to be ok."

"How bad is it?"

"Well, if you have been thanking God once a day, make it three. Your husband is one of the luckiest men I've ever seen under the circumstances, he is supposed to be dead but by a miraculous intervention he was able to make it alive. The stab wounds inflicted on him is so severe that nobody is supposed to come out of it alive. I'm afraid nothing can be done about the broken arm."

"Oh God, doctor a broken arm? How is he going to lecture again?"

"Again he is lucky. It was his left arm that got broken. But overtime, I guess he is going to be ok."

"How soon can he go back to his lecturing job?"

Well, since it is not his right arm, I would say two weeks from now. By then he should be pretty ok."

"I don't know doctor. Do you think it is wise to let him go back to his lecturing job?"

"Does he have another source of income?"

"No" she replied

"That's that then. You just let him do his thing."

"But isn't it dangerous, this people may come back if they discover he's not dead. It is obvious they wanted to kill him" she said. "There are some things men are passionate about and without it they are as good as dead men walking." The doctor said. Ok then, when is he going to be discharged?" Mrs. Muyiwa asked.

"Mmm... in one week but in the mean time take care of yourself. Everything is going to be ok."

Chapter 2

The Pyrate Confraternity, a noble fraternity of gentlemen of honour is a highly principled confraternity. It was formed by intellectuals. The aim was to fight injustice in the society especially tribal discrimination. The spiritual eye, Wole Soyinka who was a student of English and Literature as at then was a man that was rugged to the core. Because of his ruggedity, he became a professor in English and Literature. What more, he was awarded a Noble Laureate in literature. Aside that, he is manly, bold and courageous. In his days, he saw how tribal discrimination was affecting his fellow Nigerians. He wanted to put an end to it or at least reduce it. He formed an idea, had another six people sharing the same belief and before long, the Pyrate Confraternity was established by the magnificent 7; soon, the number increased to 15 to become the 15 men on a dead man's chest.

To combat tribalism within their ranks, they adopted piratical names different from their birth names. Names with no trace to any tribe or origin, thus was born the Jolly Roger Deck (University College, Ibadan, Nigeria) which, for a long time, remained the mother ship of the Pyrate Confraternity.

Over time, just like the spread of wild fire, students from other emerging higher institutions of learning began to embrace the spirit of piracy and its commitment to protect the weak in a de-tribalized Nigeria. The confraternity was open to promising students who are physically fit and among the brightest in their various departments. The spread across several campuses gave birth to the first conference which was held on mother ship JR1 in March 1973 with 140 members in attendance. Five years later when the Supreme Pyrate Council (SPC) was inaugurulated in November 1978 following a proposal made for a formal organization structure for the PC and the establishment of the SPC, the composition of the SPC was spelt out and adopted at the conference which recorded the attendance of 600 members

In 1980, the PC was formally registered with the Nigerian Federal Ministry of Internal Affair with the name National Association of Seadogs (NAS) and registration number RC 1592. By that time there were a total of 18 decks with over 22,000 individuals in PC.

Because they were highly principled, they had more to fear from their rugged brothers than the outside world. Once you were seen in campus not well dressed, you have lagged. This defect would be corrected by a certain measure; if it is known that you were in a bar during lecture hours instead of in the class, you have sinned and to straighten the person out, a penance was given to that person. If it is known you acted in ways not morally accepted by descent people in society, a penance was given. But in extreme cases like stealing or armed robbery, rape, murder or even involving oneself in thuggery , the price to pay was enormous. Then it ranges from black spotting to the ultimate which is red spotting.

When a pyrate is black spotted, he is marooned for several months. But if he is red spotted; he is thrown overboard to be carried away by the currents of the waters, figuratively speaking of course. What this means is that if he is to become a pyrate again, he has to go through the processes. And life outside the pyrate world becomes dull. The simple difference is that a black spotted dog is still a pyrate but a red spotted dog is no longer a pyrate.

Of course when a black spotted pyrate gets himself into trouble, financially or otherwise, he is not to expect any help from his rugged brothers. And again he is not to associate with his rugged brothers and if he happens to meet them by *happenstance*, he is not to claw them as a dog or use pyratical terms when communicating. There was the case of a deckhand who thought that because he was familiar with the deck officers he could be pardoned for his sin, his sin was that he was discovered in a drinking bar late in the night misbehaving because he was drunk. He was seen by another pyrate who informed the deck officers. That night around 20:00hrs when he was coming from class, seven seadogs rounded him up. He was navigated to a nearby island, hauled seriously, then placed on a black spot. The next day word was sent to all the dogs that a certain dog was on spot and on no account should he be seen affiliating with dogs. Three days later he was discovered chatting with another dog and using pyratical terms. The dog in question he was chatting with was not around when he was placed on spot; again word was sent to the deck officers about the dog placed on spot and his recent activities. The next day, he was dived again but by his close pals who were also deck officers as he was observing his siesta. He was asked if it was true that he used pyratical terms with a dog. But because they were his close pals, he started to say "Ahoy me….." one of the dogs slapped him violently that he almost lost a tooth. The same guy who slapped him also said, "Follow us." of course he had no choice than to follow them.

Confraternity or fratrenity by campus standard is more or less like a shadow. You cannot run from it. He followed them to a nearby island where he was hauled mercilessly. With that he learnt his lessons. It took three month before he was completely healed.

In the pyrate ship, drastic measures are allowed in order to enhance self discipline: "order is order" is one of the pillars of the pyrate confraternity. When orders are disobeyed then calamity ensues. The dog who refuses to obey is considered doomed. There's no telling the calamity that will befall that dog. But for just one time that it happened, it cost the pyrates dearly.

After 18:00hrs, all the deck officers as well as the deckhands were already seated. The steerer, the number one man of the pyrate ship stood up to address the seadogs present.

"Ahoy me seadogs."

"Ahoy me rugged steerer." the deckhand and the rest officers replied

"Greetings to you all and thanks for coming on such short notice. Without wasting our time, I would address the issue at hand. It is my belief that everybody on board must have heard of what happened to Prof. Muyiwa. Word on the street is that we are the ones responsible for the HIT.

Ahoy Jack sparrow, it is my belief that you know something of this matter. Kindly enlighten us as to what really happened; will you?"

In the pyrate ship, once on board, it is more or less a crime to identify a fellow dog by his lubbish name. Failure to identify a seadog by his pyratical name calls for hauling. What penance is to the Catholic Church, hauling is to the Pyrates fraternity. Ahoy Jack Sparrow of course was his pyratical name and not his lubbish name. He stood up and said:

"Ahoy me rugged steerer, Ahoy me deck officers, all other protocols observed. I a rugged seadog, doggish Ahoy Jack sparrow, a deckhand of mothership. According to Ahoy Barboosa, he said he saw Ahoy John Hawking and three other dogs in *black and black* around 18:50hrs two days ago"

"Where is Ahoy Barboosa now?" the steerer asked.

"He is having a lecture now.

"Who were the three other persons with him?"

"According to him he said he couldn't see their faces properly because it was dark."

"What about Ahoy John Hawkins, is he here?" Nobody answered.

"Ok, Ahoy Jack sparrow, continue." The steerer said.

"I don't know much except what Ahoy Barboosa told me."

"And what is that?" asked the steerer

"Ahoy Barboosa said Ahoy John Hawkins has failed Prof. Muyiwa's course twice now and that he cannot afford to fail it again. Though I don't know if that was enough to attack

Prof. Muyiwa. And I'm not saying he did. I only thought it odd that Ahoy John Hawkins and the three others with him should be in black almost the same time Prof. Muyiwa was attacked."

"Did any body pass Ahoy John Hawkins the signal for this meeting?"

"I did." Ahoy Jack sparrow said.

At that moment, a door opened and a pyrate walked in and closed the door quietly. He apologized for coming late, then found a spot to squeeze himself in. The steerer continued like nothing had happened. "Please if anybody should come across Ahoy John Hawkins inform him that he is to see the deck officers immediately for failing to come for this meeting when he was passed the signal. Meanwhile if there's anything bothering any of you, now is the time to air it out. Ahoy Captain Woods, please get the house some drinks." By the time they were through with their bottles of beer and stout, the steerer decided to address the last issue.

"Ahoy Rogers Moore, fall out." He was referring to the dog who came late.

"Ahoy Hauler, haul him for five minutes."

Ahoy Roger Moore already knew his fate. It is against the code to come late for a meeting. He wasn't worried. Hualing makes him more rugged. There were cases whereby at the end of a hauling session, the victim carried either a broken arm, or broken leg or a shaking tooth home. And in some cases it could be worse if care is not taken.

By the time the hauler was through with his thing, the steerer stood up and said;

"Ahoy seadogs!"

"Ahoy me rugged steerer" they echoed in response

"Well," the steerer continued... "It seems nothing is bothering anybody and since that's that, there's no point delaying us any longer. Sail away Ahoy seadogs"

"Sail away me rugged steerer" they echoed in response.

Ahoy John Hawkins lubbish Ade was from a rich family; over the years as a pyrate, he had contributed immensely to the poor and needy in the society. It was for this reason, more than anything else that he was inducted into the Pyrates Confraternity. *Upstairs* he had nothing, but with help of his intelligent friends he passed his exams with ease. But one thing with fortune is that it smiles, afterwards it betrays. It betrayed Ade in the sense that despite all he did to pass Prof. Muyiwa's course, he failed it. Prof. Muyiwa is so principled that he does not take bribe. Ade was willing to offer him an amount he cannot refuse but Prof. Muyiwa wasn't the type. In the end Ade had no choice but to threaten the lecturer. Little did he know that he would carry out the threat. Later when word was out that the professors was still alive, it was like a huge stone off his shoulder. He became light. He was already thinking of what to do with the blood in his hands then all of a sudden it was like the blood just cleaned off. When that was settled, it seemed a bigger problem was still on his plate. Certainly, the pyrates cannot be fooled. They were far too intelligent not to know about his involvement in the attack on the lecturer. For fear of the hauling he was going to receive, he didn't go for the meeting the day before. But he knew at the back of his mind that there was no way he was going to escape the hauling. And if truth be told that was but a small price to pay for the mortal sin he had committed. He knew that what he deserved was a red spot. But again was he not a personal friend of the steerer and some of his officers. He was thinking that certainly some few strings can be pulled. Instead of red spotting they might give him black. After all, he had done so much for the fraternity. Then all of a sudden, as if the Spirit of God visited him, he started to think—*what's the point of all these? Isn't it better to be a lubber than to be a pyrate? What good does being a pyrate do anyway? If I had been a lubber I wouldn't have had to worry about what my rugged brothers would do to me. I would have gotten away with my mortal sin but now I have to worry about my penance. If only I didn't join.* He was thinking. Maybe a red spot would be better but he knew at the back of his mind that he was deceiving himself. Something in the hood made him feel good.

Renouncing was strictly out of the question. Once the pyrates feel they have been betrayed, there's no telling what they will do to keep you shut. The thought of renunciation quickly vanished as it came. He suddenly realised that fraternity is more or less like a prison, where you have more to fear from the inmates and prison warders than from the outside world. Finally, he regretted joining a fraternity. Just as he was contemplating what to do, he heard a knock on the door of his room. Suspecting who might be at the door, he decided to see for himself. He was right.

A dog was there; and not just a dog but the 1st pettymate of the deck. For the 1st pettymate of the deck to be at his house meant trouble. But his face was expressionless when he said;

"Ahoy me deck officer, what a surprise. Come on in."

"Ahoy seadog," the 1st pettymate said "I'm sorry. I havn't the time now. Tomorrow by 18:00hrs the deck officers will be waiting for you for a brief meeting at the steerer's house."

"Ahoy me 1st pettymate, may I ask why?"

"This is an order, you don't question orders."

As he turned to leave he said "Sail away Ahoy seadog."

"Sail away me rugged deck officer." Ahoy John Hawkins responded.

Chapter 3

By the late 1960s, the pyrates had grown so much in numbers that it became difficult to carry everybody along. Naturally, factors started to develop. The spirit of brotherhood began to die. There were caucuses introduced within the organisation. According to Mario puzo, *"Power is not everything but the only thing needed to elbow your way through the difficulties of life."* And so it was that groups of seadogs began to form caucuses within the Pyrates Confraternity in order to wield power and pass it to members of their caucus. At this time, orders were no longer obeyed. Pyrates began to discriminate against pyrates. Deck officers became sentimental in their dealings with the rest of the crew. The very principles which made the Pyrates Confraternity so discrete and rugged began to fall apart. The foundation of the Pyrates Confraternity began to wobble. It was also during this period that the steerer of the pyrate's ship was forced to think of what to do to settle the numerous issues at hand. He knew very well that if the case against Ahoy John Hawkins was true, then he had no option but to red spot him after serious hauling. But then again Ahoy John Hawkins was not only his personal friend he was also a member of his caucus and what more, he had contributed greatly to charitable activities of the Pyrates. Just as he was contemplating, he heard a knock at the door. Opening it, he discovered his officers and Ahoy John Hawkins with his crew waiting. He ushered them in. Based on his ruggedity as the steerer of the deck which naturally means he must be rich. He was able to furnish the room to his taste, the room was a self-contained apartment with a kitchen, bath & W/C attached to it. There was a flowery designed fluffy carpet on the floor from wall to wall; a black and white old television set was at the corner of the room; a cassette player was also beside the television set. A 16 inches mattress was at the opposite side with a fine thick green blanket as the bed cover then; a table and chair were beside it as well for reading. The room, 16 ft by 16 ft painted in a cartoon colour was big enough to accommodate 11 persons for a meeting.

The meeting was done in the traditional way with everybody standing in a circular form.

"Ahoy me rugged seadogs," the steerer began

"Ahoy me rugged steerer" they responded.

The steerer continued,"Ahoy John Hawkins, Colombus, Calculus and Bloody Dog, fall out." They stepped out of the circle and into the circle. The steerer continued, "We have investigated the incident that happened two days ago and we now pronounce the four of you guilty of the crime. You are here to defend your actions."

"Ahoy me rugged steerer, we didn't do anything to Prof. Muyiwa." It was the 1st pettymate that replied him.

"You don't understand, there's no appeal to that judgment.

You must pay the price for the violent act carried out on Prof. Muyiwa. As you know, it is one of our objectives to deliever our fellow brothers and that is the reason we wish to hear you out."

With the measured tone of anger in his voice, the expression of one having difficulty in controlling the anger in his eyes and the determination to strike if they dare oppose him, threw Ahoy John Hawkins off grid, he decided to tell it all.

"Ahoy me deck officers," he began,

"I'm very sorry for the assault on Prof. Muyiwa. Based on the objective to deliver a fellow seadog, I ask that you pardon us." He knew very well that the steerer can pardon him but for the other three not in their caucus, he can't be sure. He was scared for them. The steerer heaved a sigh of relief. It was time to pronounce judgement. He knew what he was to do was not right but he continued anyway.

"Ahoy John Hawkins, for being brave enough to tell the truth, you are placed on a black spot; and for the rest that denied the accusation, a red spot is placed on you. Ahoy Hauler, take Ahoy John Hawkins aside and have him hauled for 20 minutes. As for lubbish Samuel, Innocent and Olalekan, you can leave us." Finally they were betrayed. Only the KMS (The killer and maker of souls) was not happy. This was injustice but he kept his face expressionless and didn't say anything.

One week later, marking the end of the session was time to anchor the position of the steerer to somebody else so that the ship can continue sailing. Although the anchoring of that position was done mainly by appointment rather than by election, but when it is obvious that the deckhands prefer

FRATERNITY

a particular dog to lead them then that dog was given the power to lead. The KMS and other dogs from steerer's caucus contested for the position. In the end, it was clear beyond doubt that the KMS was the person the deckhands wanted.

But the steerer would not have that. He wanted somebody from his caucus to be the steerer of the deck. The rift became too much that Wole Soyinka the founder, had to intervene. For some reasons he preferred the other dog contesting for the position. That was when Bolaji Carew the KMS of the deck decided on what to do.

The killer and maker of souls (K.M.S.) who is the keeper of sacred scrolls then, the most treasured item on the pyrates treasure chest, who above all others, must be loyal to the steerer, must never betray him finally decided the time has come to stand up for justice.

He was dark complexioned, 5ft 8inches tall, broad shouldered and handsome in that delicate way that is irresistible to ladies. His greatest asset was his quiet nature and his ability to keep things to himself. Bolaji Carew, because of his gentle nature was unpredictable. The steerer couldn't tell if he had a caucus of his own or if he was even interested in the caucus thing. But one thing that could be established was that Bolaji Carew had a certain kind of presence that demanded respect. Because of his unscrupulous nature, the steerer didn't know that one of the dogs he red spotted was in Carew's caucus. When Wole Soyinka proclaimed his choice, Carew decided to act fast. He called the members of his caucus and told them what he had in mind and if they were willing to back him up. They pledged their support. The next day, word was sent through the SJ and the 2nd pettymate to

25

the rest of the deck officers that Carew has backed out of the Pyrates Confraternity that he was no longer interested in sailing with the pyrates.

The steerer was mad with fury.

Immediately he sent his hauler and his 1st pettymate to go and bring the KMS. They went and came back to complain that the KMS has refused to come with them. He was mad with fury even more. He as the steerer of the deck cannot be disobeyed. It was with the effort of the other deck officers he was able to control himself. By the time he was calm enough to reason more wisely he said to the rest deck officers, "Ok if he doesn't want to sail with us then he should return our property with him." The others nodded. After all, that was the right thing to do. Later they can treat his fuck up, they told themselves. Only the 2nd pettymate and SJ were indifferent to their ideas but the steerer was too mad with fury to notice it.

The next day, the hauler and the 1st pettymate were dispatched by the steerer to go and get their scroll back. On getting to Carew's hostel, they met the 2nd pettymate and the SJ and some other dogs. Not knowing what they were doing there, they decided to get straight to the point and leave as soon as possible. The hostel was scanty with students. Most students had finished their exams and gone home, only a few had a paper or two to write or practicals to do. The hostel was a two-storey building with the KMS on the last. It was some few minutes after 18:00hrs, they said to the KMS (as politely as possible so that a scene would not be created). *"We understand you don't want to sail with us. That can be understood. The only thing we want from you is our property in your possession. Once we have that you are as free as a bird in the air.*

His reply was: *"I'm afraid I cannot give you that. I was chosen by the deckhands to steer the ship yet you've refused to give me the power. I guess I have to do what I have to do to hold on to that power."*

Seeing the resistance they decide to get tough

"Look, we don't want any trouble, just give us what we want and we'll leave you alone."

"Go tell the steerer to go to hell." The KMS said. The Hauler and 1st pettymate got to him. The Hauler slapped him hard on the face; the 1st pettymate kicked him in the stomach which made him doubled over. But that was as far as they went. The 2nd shipmate got up from where he was lying on the bed; the SJ got up too and started fighting the Hauler and 1st pettymate. The two other deckhands didn't see any reason to join in the fight but they went to the KMS and held him. The kick in the stomach had really done some damage. They made him lie on the bed. Meanwhile the fight was still going on. The 2nd pettymate was dragging them outside, but they were hitting him hard. The SJ saw what he was trying to do so he played along in dragging them outside. Finally the the 2nd pettymate was able to drag the hauler and the 1st pettymate outside. They in turn with the hauler and 1st pettymate were also trying to drag the 2nd pettymate and the SJ inside. But somehow the 2nd pettymate got an upper hand in the fight, he toppled them over the balustrade but as they were going down, they held on to him and dragged him down as well. They landed with their

heads and died instantly. With this incident, Wole Soyinka was forced to accept his loss and continue with his life while at the same time it gave birth to the rise of a new confraternity called the BUCCANEERS.

Chapter 4

Since the pyrates never wanted their name anymore stained than necessary, they decided to forgo vengeance. Wole Soyinka also accepted his fate, although he had wanted that treasured item badly for he was part of the founding fathers that wrote and signed on the original scroll. But what distressed him most was the name the new confraternity decided to call themselves. Some sourses had it that he'll never forgive that confraternity for adopting that name: The "BUCCANEERS." In the Pyrates Confraternity, the Buccaneers were dogs who had achieved great success in their respective field of studies. It also meant dogs who had achieved victory in the business empire. Dogs who were financially independent, infact it meant victorious dogs. And so when Carew won the position of the steerer but was refused him, he had no option but to take along with him the original scroll written and signed by Wole Soyinka and six other dogs. When he became victorious in keeping that scroll for himself despite that some lives were lost, he had no option again but to adopt the name BUCCANEERS.

Another reason Bolaji Carew, the founder of the

Buccaneers Confraternity adopted that name was because, according to legend, Buccaneers were those rarest of men who were extraordinarily brave. Men who chose to stand up for justice no matter the cost they have to pay, even if they have to sacrifice their lives for the cause. Of course they were also pyrates but they chose to attack only Spanish ships at sea, unlike the other pyratres who attacked any ship at sea whether from their own country or not.

The Buccaneers of legend chose to attack only Spanish ships because in the world as at the 17th century, Spain the world power as at then was exploiting countries less powerful. It happened that the West Indies, the place the Buccaneers settled was one of the countries exploited. In revenge, they choose to attack Spanish ships at sea; especially in the Caribbean seas, to recover what has been stolen from them, as well as any other treasure they needed for survival.

In 1972, after the founding fathers have settled such things like symbols and emblem, initiation rites and ceremonies, language and structure of organization, the Buccaneer's Confraternity became a formal organisation to be reckoned with in the University College Ibadan, Ibadan, Nigeria.

They were seen as the best dressed group of students in the school. In their departments, they were counted among the best five in their classes. Their manner of approach was so impressive to the extent that the most beautiful girls in the campus took it as a previledge or honour to sleep with them. At the end of every semester, they would organize a party were a busload of beautiful girls were brought. In no distant time, because of the way they carried themselves, the school authority made them to be the watch dogs to check-mate illegal activities going on inside the campus. Thay became so exceptional in everything they do that they were nicknamed "fine boys". In no distant time every guys' wish was to be a Buccaneer.

In the early eighties, the scene became so barbaric as new confraternities emerged. Fraternities wanting to make a name for themselves involved themselves in violent and criminal acts creating and instilling fear among campus students. In no time, the timid ones who wanted protection and power began to join these fraternities. It was around this time the Pyrates, not wanting to associate themselves with the evil perpetuated by the new generation fraternities decided to leave the scene for them. It was because of the criminal acts carried out by these fraternities that every fraternities was termed "secret cult."

In the 1980s, fraternities spread throughout the over 300 institutions of higher education in the country then. The Neo-Black Movement of Africa" (also called the Black Axe) emerged from the University of Benin in Edo State, while the Supreme Eiye Confraternity (also known as the National Association of Air Lords) originated in Ibadan in 1969. Students at the University of Calabar in Cross River State, founded the External Fraternal Order of the Legion Consortium (the Klansmen Konfraternity), while a former member of the Buccaneer Confraternity, not meeting with expected standard as expected, was yellow spotted. He went on to found the Supreme Vikings Confraternity (the Adventurers or alternately, the Norse Men Club of Nigeria). In the early 1990s, as the end of the second republic drew near, fraternity activities expanded dramatically especially in the Niger Delta region. It was during this period the Family Confraternity (also known as the Mafia) which modeled itself after the Italian Mafia emerged.

The Brotherhood of the Blood (also known as Two-Two or Black Baret) another notorious fraternity was founded at Enugu State University of Science and Technology.

The fraternities established in the early 1990s are legion. They included Second Son of Satan (sss), Night Cadet, Mgba Mgba Brothers, Temple of Edon, Trojan horse, Jurists, White Bishops, Gentlemen Clubs, The Executioners, Black Scorpion, Red Sea Horse, Maphite and many more.

In the late 1990s, all female fraternities began to emerge. These include Black Brassiere (Black Bra), the Viqueens, Daughters of Jezebel, the Damsel and Pink Ladies.

As pyrates, one of their major abilities is weather the storms, so that the ship does not capsize. Before initiation, screening tests are carried out three times to see if the lubbers intending to be pyrate are fit to be pyrates. But over time, they lost that ability. And so if was the buccaneers that carried on with that virtue. And so while the pyrates left the scene, the Buccaneers choose to stay. It was during this period the slogan "every dog has a master and the master is the Lord" came out. For while the pyrates were referred to as seadogs, the Buccaneers were referred to as SeaLords. But in the end, the Buccaneers will also find themselves wanting to leave the scene for it became too barbaric.

In the early 90s, when cultism was so rampant everybody was on the watch out for *who is who*. Even the smallest among them whom one might think as *nobody* cannot be underestimated. In most cases, it was the smallest ones that usually emerge as the *Don of a confraternity*. A decade later, some 30 years after the Buccaneers Confraternity was founded, at the University of Benin, Benin City, Desmond Okogie, who was the big eye of the Buccaneers ship that is, the number one man of the Buccaneers Confraternity at deck levels was a much disciplined man. Part of his *Ruggedity* was that he was too disciplined. Lagging deckhands were hauled seriously to make them more rugged for the dangerous times ahead. He was 5 ft 8inches tall, dresses in a way that appealed to the opposite sex, dark in complexion, with mediun size eyes, nose and mouth. Academically, he was intelligent. The fact of the matter is, there was more to him than meets the eyes. A man named Jackson Ogbegbor, an Axeman, had been harassing him, provoking him to a fight but Desmond was more than that. One of his assets was his ability to stay out of troubles. At first, Jackson was intimidated by Desmond's physical appearance. Beautiful girls of his department tend to flock around Desmond. Aside his handsomeness, Desmond was intelligent and so it was natural that in the process of teaching the dull girls in his department, they fall temporally in love with each other and before one can say Jack Bauer they were already in bed. But Jackson was jealous of this. He didn't have the *swag* to sway girls to bed. He did his things roughly. He couldn't dress neatly; most times his shirts were soiled with stains of different kinds. While Desmond was getting girls cheap, it was difficult for Jackson to *screw* a girl in a semester. Most times, he raped girls with the help of his squad. It was typical of the Axemen as at that time. Another thing was that while others in class showed him some certain kind of respect, Desmond on the other hand didn't care if he was anything of value. As a matter of fact, he showed Jackson contempt on many occasions when they come across each other, Jackson would hit him with his shoulder as they brush pass each other hoping that Desmond would turn around and ask him or try to show that he was brave. But Desmond would smile and let it go. Desmond tended to know his frustration.

It happened that there was a girl named Ivie Amadason, a beautiful average sized young girl of 21 and 5'5" tall. She had big eyeballs that tended to attract men towards her. Her nose was perfectly molded, her mouth and lips so tantalizing that one finds himself fighting the urge not to kiss her. Her curves were so dramatic that one cannot pass her by without giving her a second look. Her bust tended to be struggling to get out of her blouse. Her *ass,* although not too large it was something that got men's attention. To crown it all, she was fair complexioned.

Out of protection, she chose to be the girlfriend of Jackson. Of course, it was a well known fact that Jackson was a cultist and arrogant. Rumour had it that if a beautiful girl carries herself too much and not allow them {Axemen} to flirt with her, they would rape her. Although she allowed Jackson to buy her things and take her out on dates she did not sleep with him. She lied to him that she was still a virgin and would wish to keep it till marriage. Jackson, head over heels in love with her would not push it further. She seemed to know she had powers over him and she used it to control the situation of things.

On a certain day when she was on her way to school, she

heard somebody say behind her "Hello cutie, do you know you would look great with two pounds less?"

Turning around, she found Desmond behind her and smiled. She had always liked Desmond because of the way he carried himself. But Desmond seemed to be the only one who didn't care about her beauty. Smiling she asked:

"How am I going to do that?"

"In my opinion, your clothes weigh exactly two pounds; if you take them off you would see what I'm talking about. I would like to see how great you would be with your clothes off."

She had to laugh because Desmond seemed funny to her; she loved the approach and thought if wouldn't be a bad idea to sleep with him.

"Hmn, Desmond" she continued "I have failed my G.S.T course two times now. Do you think you can put me through?"

"Of course, just lemme know when will be good for you. when I get home I will look for my...?"

"Don't worry, I'll bring mine." She interrupted him.

"Will tomorrow evening be ok for you?" she asked. He smiled like he has discovered a gold mine.

"Are you kidding me? Tomorrow is a public holiday for me." He said

"Ok then, five in the evening," she said and she diverted to her block where she receives her lectures.

The following day, when she came back from her lectures, around 16:00 hrs, she was sweating profusely. She dropped her bag, stripped herself naked and went into the bathroom. After some fifteen minutes when she was satisfied that she was thoroughly clean, she stepped out. The room was a self contained room with all the necessary facilities available for accommodation. She thought of what to put on to seduce her host. She thought of an average sized skirt with a tight bluse that would reveal her figure, but then she thought that that would be too forward and not persuasive enough. She thought of a mini skirt and a blouse that would expose some parts of her milky breast but then she would look more like a whore in the streets. Finally, she settled for a low waist jeans that would expose her *ass* a little any moment she bends; and a little top that would expose her navel and a jacket to cover it up. After the application of her cosmetics and wearing of her dress, she looked herself in the mirror again, she couldn't help it but smile; then she thought: *even the priest of God, a reverened father, would not think twice to strip himself naked to have me.*

By the time she got to Desmond's place, it was 16:55 hrs. She only had to knock once when the door was flung wide open.

When he saw her, he was flabbergasted: he couldn't help it but ask "How was heaven when you left it?"

"Are you going to leave me here?" she asked

"Oh my heaven, come on in"

"Where am I going to hang this jacket?" she demanded.

"Oh, let me take it."

Just as he was pulling off her jacket, he couldn't help but perceive the cologne she was wearing. It was so nice to the extent of reminding him of foods of similar aroma. Pulling off her second arm, and a few inches behind her, he noticed that she was wearing a low waist jeans and to make matters worse, she was not wearing her panties. Knowledge of that got his dick excited that it grew extra inches instantly.

"Sit down here." he showed her where to sit and went to the fridge to bring out two cans of Coke-cola drink.

"Your apartment is so nice. Do you live here all alone?"

"Yes. But trust me, sometimes I get so bored."

"Don't you have a girl friend?"

"Since we had a fight, we've not been able to resolve it. The problem is long distance, it is killing the relationship."

"You need a girl around here to be keeping you company."

"Yeah.", he gave her a can of coke while he opened one himself

"I will think about it. Did you bring your G.S.T textbook?"

"Yeah; it's in my bag, let me go get it" Just as she bent down to pick up the book from her bag, some part of her *ass* showed; and from that moment on, he couldn't think straight anymore. By the time she was coming back to her seat, he was having trouble repressing his *dick* from excitement. She noticed it and smiled but Desmond felt shy.

"Hey dolly I'm not comfortable on the table I'm sitting on. Do you mind if we go to the bed, I mean no offence?" He said.

"Of course, by all means." She replied.

As they were sitting on the bed, side by side with their back against the wall, he asked her.

"Which of the topics is giving you trouble?"

"Philosophy and logic."

Just as she said that, her hand went to his lap, of course to prepare for the occasion. He was wearing a fine pair of blue boxers, which enabled her hand to probe deeper. He couldn't resist her .He turned to face her and kissed her on the lips.

It was a sweet sensual kiss. It went on for a time, they were exploring each other with their tongues. Soon she removed her blouse to expose her milky breasts. When Desmond saw them, he was speechless. The kissing continued, soon he went to her breasts and started caressing them. His tongue went to one of her boobs while one of his hands was on the other; and instantly her nipples grew. Soon she started to unbutton her trousers; because of the excitement she had trouble removing it but he noticed her trouble and so helped her out. Finally she was stripped of her trousers. Then she went to him to remove his boxers. This time around his *dick* was already hard and she loved it. They continued fondling each other. After a while when she was wet she took his dick to her mouth and started sucking it. This was the part he enjoyed most when making love. The part that makes him care less if Jesus Christ is coming again. When he was satisfied, he bent to enter her. At first gently, but then the ride picked up gear and that was when she started moaning confusing sounds. After a long while, he dismounted her.

On hearing the score of Desmond with his girlfriend, Jackson's mind went numb. He couldn't think of anything. Then like the rising sun, rage started to grow in him. One thing was certain: Desmond must pay for his crime.

The motto of the Axemen is: *Forgiveness is a sin*. You don't *fuck* with the Axemen and go free, especially when you are a Jew. A Jew is a term for used for someone who is not a member of their fraternity. It was this slogan, *forgiveness is a sin* that earned them their notoriety.

On January 10, 1999, one of the most notable single

attack occurred at Obafemi Awolowo University (OAU) in Ife, Osun state. OAU had been considered one of the safest universities in the country, largely due to students organized resistance to fraternities. After one fraternity member was shot and killed in an attempted kidnapping in 1991, the activities of fraternities tended to subside. But in February 1999, because of a tip from a student to the Students' Union Government about certain students threatening other students, the students' leaders organized a campus wide search which led to the capture of eight fraternity members who were members of the Black Axe Confraternity. Their sin was that they were stock pilling machine guns and other weapons in their dorm room. This enraged the Neo-Black Movement aka Black Axe, who organized a murder squared that hacked the Students' Union secretary general to death in his bed and targeted other students' leaders.

In the University of Benin, Benin City, Edo State the place of their origin, they were so notorious to the extent that they don't mind warring three different fraternities at the same time all in the name of "this is our territory you cannot take if from us."

One of their virtues that is, if you can call it a virtue, is that they are never tired of fighting. Fighting itself is not bad, it becomes a virtue when you are fighting for a just cause. In other words, it is good to fight so long as it is for a just cause. It can be said that they are haters of peace. Hardly any semester goes by without them oppressing or provoking somebody to fight them. Although the initiatial goal of the fraternity was to fight against oppression anywhere it is existing, they later came to see the pleasure of oppressing. To most of them, it was the highest pleasure.

1999 was the year their fame escalated. In the early 90's when fraternities was thriving, a new confraternity called Maphite raised their flag in the waters of Edo State University, Ekpoma. Rumour has it that they broke away from the Mafia Confraternity. Others said they came out from the Black Axe Confraternity. In any case, they modeled themselves after military order. They gave ranking officers military titles and use military terms when communicating with each other. It was only natural that green should be the colour they associate themselves with. Because they were so military, they were organized. Over the years, their reputation for ruggedity became pronounced. It was then the Axemen took note of them and wondered: *who the hell are these set of people that call themselves Maphites?*

And so it was that they became a force to be reckoned with and not to be taken for granted. In the year 1999, it became so much that the Axemen began to see them as their rival.

In their opinion, since they originated from Benin City, the capital of Edo State, it therefore means that Edo State is their territory and not to be shared by any rival. And so as it was natural with them, they started provoking members of the Maphite Confraternity into a fight. But the Maphites knew better than to engage in a war with the NBM. Not necessarily out of fear but because they want to graduate and move on to the next stage of improving their society with what they have read in school. But one thing led to another and before one can say Jack Bauer a member of the Maphite Confraternity was shot dead in the streets of Ekpoma.

The Maphites did their investigation and discovered the Black Axe to be responsible for the HIT.

Sun Tzu, a Chinese writer once said that, "If you know your enemy, you need not fear a hundered battles."

The Maphites happen to know that the only way to win a war is to try to know the prey completely and then get the enemy down with everything they've got. Another advantage they got was their ability to keep themselves low key. For while the Axe men were fond of *casting* themselves feeling that they were superior, making everybody know them, the Maphites on the other hand knew the advantage of being not known, and so while the Maphites knew a lot of the Axemen and where they hang out, the Axemen knew only a few of the Maphites and the Maphites were not exactly much.

The next day, three Axemen were enjoying themselves. This could be seen from the fact that they were all laughing hilariously completely unaware of two men walking to the bar. As a matter of fact there was nothing to reveal out of the two men. They were casual, they didn't look like people who could hurt a fly. They were moving casually and smoking their cigarettes. But as soon as they got to where the three axemen were drinking they opened fire on them. Instantly the three Axemen died. And so the war of 1999 started. The Axemen, believing that *forgiveness is a sin* didn't see the need for peace and the Maphite believing in *no retreat, no surrender* in war made the matter a strong tangle. It was so intense that both parties lost a lot of their members, but the Axemen had more to loose because they were many.

According to Wole Soyinka in his book *The Man Died* wrote: "In time of war, no man is completely innocent."

Mr. Okogie was a man whom God had blessed so much. He graduated with a 1ˢᵗ class honours in Medical Laboratory and immediately the University Teaching Hospital of Edo State University employed him. In no distant time. He was able to rent an apartment and furnish it. He bought a car and finally, he fell in love with a lady and got married. The marriage produced three beautiful children. Two boys and a girl.

To him life was good. A beautiful wife and three lovely children.

What could be better than this? He thought.

Every now and then he kept thinking and reflecting on how God has been good to him even right from his University days. Despite the fact that he was not the best of Christians.

Way back in school, he was a Maphite. Although, he was rugged enough to be the number one man, that is the General of the Maphite Confraternity, he declined because of his love for academics. Now he realized what a good choice he had made and how God has blessed him for it. He began to see the necessity of breaking loose because, if truth be told, the fraternity wasn't doing him any good and moreover he didn't want any harm to come to his family. He didn't think himself to be in any danger since he graduated a long time ago.

He thought of the war that was going on and felt sorry for the members of his fraternity that must have died. He realized that there was no point joining a fraternity afterall. He felt safe from the fact that nobody knew him and moreover he was in a new place at Irrua, some 30 kilometres from Ekpoma, where nobody knew him. And so he felt safe and continued with his normal routine of going to work and coming back in the evening.

Meanwhile the Axemen were loosing their members. They were frustrated, they din't like it that they couldn't get a single Maphite down. It became so intense that road blocks were mounted to see if any Maphite would be running from campus. This way, they got down a lot of Maphites who couldn't stand the war. Who felt the heat was becoming too much. The majority of the Maphites were in the bush, they strategized from there, strike and returned. This way too, they were getting down a lot of the Axemen.

Consequetly the Axemen were not happy, they were frustrated because the Maphites were hitting their top men. The number one man began to think of what he was going to do to even the score. He called the chief butcher, the number three man of the fraternity, the man responsible for the carrying out the HITs. He said "AYE Axeman" the butcher replied "Aye me Axeman".

Since the initial goal of the fraternity was to fight against oppression, they themselves had to practice the act of equality. And so, among the top men they were equal while floor members were also equal regardless of the year one became a member of the fraternity- so that if one had spent ten years in the game he was equal with the one who was newly initiated so long as he was not one of the top seven.

The number one man continued, "Aye butcher, is your brother not a Maphite?"

"Yes he is." The butcher replied

"What is his position in the confraternity?" The butcher was worried with the question coming from his chief.

"He is the chief executioner of their confraternity." He replied.

The number one chuckled and said "Start plotting his map, we have to get him down."

The chief executioner is the number three man of the Maphite's Confraternity in school level. He is also responsible for the planning and hitting of civilians as it is called in their fraternity. A civilian is a person who is not a member of their fraternity.

This time around the butcher was scared. He said "Aye me Axeman, with all due respect, I cannot plot the death of my own blood brother." The number one looked at him with a menacing eye and said, "Have you forgotten the oath you swore to? Don't you know the objectives of this fraternity comes first? It is either you plot his death or we plot your death."

That moment the chief butcher regretted that he joined a fraternity. He realised that the fraternity he joined was nothing but a cult, then he realized he was in bondage.

Mrs. Okogie was dressing her kids for school that morning. She loved them all. They were so sharp and quick witted. In school they were doing averagely as expected of kid their age.

She was dressing up her second child, a girl named Andre, she was so happy that God has blessed her with this beautiful child. Just as she was wearing her sandals, the door opened and her husband came in.

"Good morning daddy." his daughter said.

"Good morning sweetie." Mr. Okogie replied.

"What happened yesterday daddy? I was going to show you what I did yesterday at school."

"Yeah? So what did you learn at school yesterday?"

"How to write, daddy"

"So what did you write?"

"Oh, I don't know, you know my Aunty has not taught us how to read yet"

Her father laughed. "Ok, if you come from school today, I will teach you how to read, ok?"

"Ok dad." the litte girl said.

Her mum was smiling when she said "Honey, you better be home in time to teach her how to read."

Mr. Okogie loved his wife so much and was really sorry that he didn't come home in time. He said, "Honey, I'm so sorry we had a lot of work to do." His wife finished dressing her kid then said "Ok, now that all is settled, let's go to the dining table for our breakfast."

Having dropped his Kids at school, he reversed to go to his place of work. But every morning he would stop at this newspaper vendor to buy the ealy morning papers.

Just as he stopped, three men dressed in black came from behind him to the driver's side of the car. Seeing them, he was about to ask if there was any thing he could do for them but at that moment, one of the boys drew a locally made pistol gun shot him in the head. Mr. Okogie's last thought was that *he had failed his family*.

Both parties became wearied from fighting. They have

lost a lot of their members, they were tired of hiding in fear, hiding in the bush, afraid to come out in the open. This time around the school was closed and everybody sent home. When the Maphites heard that one of their old members who now had a family had been shot, they decided that the war was irrelevant and pointless, that there was no sense in it anymore. They questioned, why an innocent man should be shot for nothing. A man with a family. They were forgetting that *in time of war no man is completely innocent.* So they told themselves: *enough is enough, let's call for a truce.* They arranged a place where both parties would feel safe. Since the Maphites were the once calling for the truce they were there first. Every one of them (three in number) were holding white handkerchief to signify that they want peace. But for precautionary purpose, many of their men were hidden around the vicinity. The Axemen not trusting the Maphites decided to arm themselves to the meeting. The top three men of their confraternity drove to the place shortly afterwards. Both parties were extremely cautious, none wanted to be taken unaware. To cut the long story short, a gun was found among one of the Axemen and immediately, the number one man of the Axemen fraternity was grabbed. The other two were rounded up. But the Maphites were trigger happy soldiers, they didn't bother to waste time. The two rounded up were shot immediately.

The number one man, because of the position he was holding had armed himself with charms so that when a gun is shot at him, it will not penetrate or if a cutlass were used to cut him it will bounce or even when he is poured acid, it will not burn him. And so when all these things were used in their attempt to kill him, none worked. But when one's time to die has come nothing stops it. The general of the Maphite Confraternity said: "Tie him to the vehicle they used in coming" Immediately he was tied. For the Maphites, it was a prize worth displaying. They drove him round the town of Ekpoma. By the time they were satisfied that everybody had seen their victory, they stopped. But by that time, the Axemen number one has long given up the ghost. He couldn't withstand the pothole, the mud, even the mud waters he had to drink in those streets that were water logged. It seemed there is no charm against the rough tarred roads. He was disfigured beyond recognition and he died a miserable death. For the Maphites, it was a sarvory victory. It was during this period the news came up on CNN that Edo State University, Ekpoma was the second most violent university in the world after a university in China. Shortly afterwards, the name of the school was changed to Ambrose Alli University, Ekpoma, Edo state.

"So who is this guy?" one of Jackson's squad asked. They were in a bar at Ekosodi in Uniben.

They were four in number. Each was holding a ciggy which they greedily drew from. From the look on their faces none was happy with the news they just heard. In their opinion, *how can a Jew treat an Axeman so disrespectfully?* Jackson answered; "He is in my department. For some time now, he has not been showing me the respect due me in the class." One of the boys who was impatient with small talk asked, "Where does he live?"

"He lives at Osasogie." Jackson replied.

"Then it is simple. All we have to do is pay him a visit." one of the boys said.

That evening at about 19:00hrs, the four guys went straight to Desmond's house. But unfortunately, Desmond wasn't in. Paranoid, they scattered his house, destroyed his electronics and left a note that he should leave the school if he loves his life.

When Dersmond came back, he did not have to go to an oracle to known who did it. Immediately he knew whose handwork it was. Quickly, he called his 1st shipmate to arrange a meeting for only the deck masters. In the meeting, they all concluded that no serious harm has been done and if the Akites {akite, a term used by the Buccaneers for the word Axemen} can pay for the damages, they the Buccaneers would forgo any vengeance they were supposed to carry out. And so the message was relayed to the Axemen excos.

"What are we gonna do?" the Axemen excos were asking themselves. They were in the room of their chief, the king of the castle. The chief named Osagiede was worried. They just squashed a beef with the tingos that is, the 'Eiyes' and it was uncertain if they have really accepted to let peace reign.

"What really caused this? And why did the Buccaneers link it to us?" Osagiede asked.

"Let us ask the house and if any one admits doing it then he should pay for the damages himself." one of them said.

"What if no one admits doing it?" another asked.

"Then we tell the Buccaneers we are not responsible, we'll wait and see what happens." The number two man of the house replied. Osagiede was worried. He had this kind of *what-are-you-people-yakking-about* expression on his face.

He said, "This people are unscrupulous, you can't predict them. They are not like the rest who retaliate immediately when struck a blow." The chief butcher who was the number three man of the house said; "We can handle them any day, anytime."

"Tell the rest to watch their backs and be observant. They are not to loose guard." Osagiede concluded it. And so when the house was asked, nobody admitted doing anything and they left it at that and told the Buccaneers they are not responsible.

On the third day after the Buccaneers had been notified, Jackson was to go the market to buy some food ingredients. Already, a certain kind of fear had enveloped him now that he knew that Desmond was not a Jew but as a matter of fact, the big eye of the Buccaneers Confraternity. He now realized the reason why Desmond has never been scared of him. But he thought to himself, *Desmond cannot really be that danger-ous, he plays with everyone in class, he jokes, he laughs, he is not as hot tempered as he ought to be being the big eye.*

But Jackson was not to know that an easy going nature like that was an added advantage. He thought to himself again: *these people are always rolling for peace, they don't have the guts to fight. They avoid it at all cosst. So there is really noth-ing to fear.*

He was very confident when he left his hostel. He didn't bother to be observant and so when he mounted a bike to go to the market, unknown to him, three men mounted bikes and followed him. When he dismounted the bike at the market, he was surprised to find himself rounded up by three unknown men. He wasn't given the chance to speak or even run, immediately, one of the men stabbed him on the shoulder, as he was going down, he felt the rain of blows and kicks on him, one of the men took a bottle from a nearby woman selling kerosene and burst the bottle on Jackson's head. It was serious but not fatal. The big eye's order was for him to sustain enough injury so that the money he needed to treat himself would equate the damage the Axemen were supposed to pay for.

The big eye of the Buccaneer's Confraternity ordered another meeting. The signal was passed to all deckhands. In the meeting the big eye told them to abadon ship for some few days and when the coast is clear, he would send the signal to resume sailing.

Immediately the Akites got word of what had happened to their brother, they went mad. It took the excos some extraordinary effort to calm them. As far as the word terrific goes, these men were terrific.

Being that they were equal, they don't wait for orders before they act. But the excos tend to know their pain and so he gave the order to roll.

The 1st day, they couldn't find any Buccaneer in campus. The second day their search was in vain. The third day, the same, until a week later when one of them was discovered.

The Buccaneer in question travelled before the whole saga started. And so when he was coming he didn't bother to call and ask what the Intel on the deck was. That same evening, a squad of five men rounded him up in his hostel. After they have bloodied him, they shot him in the head to make sure he was dead. When it was confirmed, they left.

In cases like this, each fraternity would send out a spy to check if the victim was their own. When the Buccaneers discoverd the victim was theirs, they squashed the beef to let peace reign.

The big eye ordered for a meeting. When all were present, he addressed them saying: "Alora SeaLords, though the sea may be rough and the tides high, we've all agreed that the treasure must be found."

The Sealords present were mad with fury for what had happened to their brother. But they must hear what the big eye had to say.

The big eye continued; "I regret the misfortune that has happened, may the soul of our R.B find peace with God."

Hearing this, they echoed their response. The big eye paused to look at everybody then continued, "It is my duty as the big eye to steer all rugged Sealord to Treasure Island. For the essence of becoming a Sealord is to discover that treasure which is out there."

Again, the Buccaneers echoed their response "I want to enjoin you all," the big eye continued, "to go back to your studies and do as if nothing had happened. Let's maintain the peace we've called for. Three weeks from now our first semester exams will start. I don't want anybody missing his exams. There's no excuse for us not to read and write our exams well."

But this wasn't what the deckhands wanted to hear. They wanted vengeance so they started agitating.

"Alora SeaLord" the big eye continued, "I know how it is. Believe me, if it were necessary I'll take my squard with me for rolling though a big eye is not suppose to involve himself with HITs but have we forgetten our principles. Don't we re-member that *no price, no pay* is still our highest policy? I feel your pain but we are not going to give them the satisfaction of knowing when we are going to strike." He concluded by saying, "Revenge is a dish best eaten cold."

With this, their fury seemed to calm down and they echoed their response. "Sail on alora me rugged brothers." The big eye bided them. The deckhands responded in their own fashion and left as the meeting came to an end.

Chapter 5

The Big eye was thinking, *there's something about rock music.* Their lyrics tend to make one reflect on life. Now he had to appreciate Stained for the lyrics he used in this track tittled, "So Far Away" at first, he couldn't understand the lyrics of the song then he replayed it again before he grabbed what Stained was singing. Simply put, Staind is so happy with the succss he has made that if it is a dream, he doesn't want to wake up and nobody should shake him in this sleep, Desmond couldn't help but think that hard work pays. Already he had plans of what to do to make so much money in the future. Money to take care of himself and the world around him, while Desmond was contemplating on the song playing, suddenly a knock came on the door. When he opened the door, he was surprised to find the KMS. The big eye doesn't have to be told that something is wrong.

"Alora me K" the big eye said.

"What brings you here?"

"Alora me eye" the KMS responded.

"One of our rugged brothers has been kidnapped. The one coming out for president in the Students' Union

Government."

The big eye was distressed when he asked;

"And who did this?"

"The Bird boys." the KMS replied.

The KMS couldn't be sure but he thought he saw something of a smile flash across the big eye's face. He couldn't believe what he heard next from the big eye.

"Kidnap one of their ranking men before we start negotiating for the release of our brother."

The National Association Of AirLords also known as the Eiye Confraternity nicknamed by other frats as the 'Bird Boys', was a fraternity known for their ferocity. They originated from the west in 1969. The word 'Eiye' is a Yoruba word for bird. It was for this reason they were nicknamed *Bird Boys*. As a result, most of their terms were associated with birds; for instance the school which they originated from is coded the mother nest. Other schools became names of big trees like iroko, mahogany, obeche and the like. Ranking men were given names of birds according to their importance. What the big eye was to the Buccaneers Confraternity aka Sealords, Ibaka was to the Eiye Confraternity aka AirLords.

Their fame for ferocity started to grow when they had fracas with a confraternity called Brotherhood of the Blood aka Blood Brothers. It was a confraternity that started in the Eastern part of Nigeria but like all others, they had to spread to other parts of the country. Just as they were trying to gain grounds in Obafemi Awolowo University, Ife, one thing led to another and before one can say Jack bauer, a baby bird was bloodied by the blood brothers. A baby bird is a newly hatched inductee in the Eiye Confraternity.

Although the blood brothers were few at the time, how they could be fished out from thousands of frat men was a thing of wonder. What could be confirmed was that the following morning three corpses of blood brothers was found at the school gate for everyone to see. There was no doubt in the minds of all, that it was the Bird Boys that was responsible for the hit.

On another occasion, the Vikings with them (the Bird Boys) were having beef in Owo Polytechnic of Ondo State. After a one month war, with both parties loosing a lot of their members, the AirLords finally got an upper hand. It is rumored that the Eiyes do a lot of charm. But how they were able to get the number one man of the Vikings Confraternity nobody knew. What happened next was a thing of shock. The head of the number one man of the Vikings Confraternity was cut off from the body and hanged in front of the school gate.

And so little by little their ferocity started to spread across the country. But for them, fraternity activities would not have flourished in the streets of Benin City, Edo state. The Axemen have always prided themselves to be the most rugged in terms of violence, but when the birdies entered the scene, they began to see themselves as followers of mother Theresa. It all started when the Airlords began to initiate unworthy people into the fraternity. People who were not undergraduates or graduates were considered unworthy. When the founding fathers founded the fraternity, it was limited to only universities and polytechnics. But as new confraternities began to spring up and for want of more members, they started inducting students from secondary or high schools. And so while other fraternities were initiating students from high schools, the Pyrates and Buccaneers initiated students from only universities and polytechnics.

These students, for want of proof that they are rugged started causing troubles hoping it'll result to a fight. Cult wars in the initial stage was fought only in the campuses. But as time went on, people were desperate for blood especially the Airlords. The AirLords wanted to prove to the Axemen that they are supreme. The Axemen wanted to prove to the Airlords that you can't fight and win somebody in his territory. And so for the most foolish of reasons, there was always war between these two frats.

It was rumoured that what ever good that was left in the Axemen (that is, if ever there was any good) it was ruined by the tingos. The Bird Boys is popularly known as tingos in the south-south region of the country particularly Edo state.

In the early stage of their fights, the Axemen were doing them more harm than they to the axemen. Then it was still a campus thing. But as the tingos began to initiate all and sundry, they began to hit the akites where it hurts.

There was a case of the number three man of the Eiye Confraternity in University of Benin who was shot dead in his hostel in B.D.P.A Uniben. The blow was too devastating that all hell broke loose. It became an all out war between the tingos and the akites. The next day the tingos who felt they are cut out from the action: that is the bus drivers, bus conductors, mechanics, and electricians even the secondary school students organized themselves into murder squads. That day the tingos were able to confirm three akites dead.

These were Axemen who felt the school was too hot for them. They decided to seek refuge in their parents' houses. But there was the case of an unfortunate incident. The particular racketeer in question was an akites; he was the kind of racketeer that likes to keep a low profile. His family didn't know anything about the other side of the life he was living. His only brother who he was closest to didn't know anything at all. It was a credit on his part but one can never tell how the wind of misfortune is going to blow. When he learnt that some of his rugged brothers have been shot dead in their houses, he decided to leave the house perhaps to travel to a nearby state until the heat has subsided. And so that was how he arranged a bag and temporally abandoned his house. Shortly after he left, some tingos assembled in front of his house. They have been hearing rumours about him but they weren't sure and so they made a few more calls to confirm the identity they are after. When it was confirmed they decided not to waste time. They went straight to the house and when they knocked, the brother of the person they are after came out to answer them. When they saw him, he fitted nicely to the description they've been trying to confirm on the phone. Immediately, one of them shot him in the chest four times. There was no way he could survive it, he died instantly. When it was confirmed, they left the scene. That same day a call was made to the Axeman the tingos were supposed to hit to tell him his brother has been shot. This was from his rugged brothers. The father who was having a heart problem, fainted and was in a coma for three days after he was told.

The akite in question when he came home later, opened up to his parents that he was a mamber of a fraternity, that it was him they were supposed to kill and that now his life is in danger unless he flies to a new place. He was sent to relatives in another state to start his university education afresh.

When the tingos later learnt that it was the wrong person they had killed, they didn't feel any remorse. For them, ruthlessness is the key to victory.

The Buccaneers in those days were the ones behind the scene. Because they were financially rugged, they were able to fix themselves in political positions in the school. For almost five sessions then, they emerged as presidents of the Student Union Government (SUG) in UNIBEN. In that way, they are able to deal with their enemies legitimately. Over the years people came to know the value of such a position especially the frat men, it became a position worth killing for. The Airlords this time, were becoming more infamous. In anything they wanted their own way. When a member made his intention known to the house to come out for the presidency they cheered him and encouraged him. In their opinion, it is about time they ruled the school and oppress their enemies.

And so it was that the Buccaneer coming out for the post of the president was issued a note of death threat on the grounds that he must pin down and not continue with his campaign if he desires to live. When he showed the note to his rugged brothers they told him they've got his back that he had nothing to worry about but to continue with his campaign. When the Airlords observed that he didn't take the threat serious and that all the corners of the school were echoing his name they decided that *enough is enough*. All they had to do was to observe him for some few days. When they discovered his routine it become easy to kidnap him. Every evening around 19:00hrs to 19:30 hrs, he followed a particular road to the class to read. On that particular evening after taking care of the other businesses he decided to go to the class and read as usual. Half way down the road, three large men approached him.

"Hey, we want to see you." They demanded

"Who are you?" he asked them.

"See, we don't want any trouble, we promise not to hurt you if you cooperate with us." the same person still answered him.

At the mention of hurt he knew the men were not playing. He was looking at them one after the other. But they seem to know what he was thinking and the men rounded him up more closely so as there won't be space for him to run. Seeing this, his next move was to make a show of bravery, but when he saw one of them flashed a gun, he knew better than to be brave. His blood chilled like a lizard in cold weather. Then he said; "Let's go."

They took him to a nearby car and drove off. It was dark and so the passers by didn't know what was happening. It was the next morning the KMS of the deck was aware that their presidential aspirant was missing. That was when he went to the big eye to tell him that their presidential aspirant has been kidnapped.

Although the business of kidnapping wasn't strange to the KMS, he was only surprised because the big eye had said "kidnap one of their ranking birds" in a way that suggests that if the worse gets to the worst, then it was going to be an all out war between them (the Sealords and the Airlords) disregarding the fact that not long ago, they squashed a beef with the Axemen on the grounds that exams are fast approaching. What he didn't know was that the big eye as a personality has lost a great deal of respect by refusing to hit back the Axemen for the loss of their rugged brother; that the big eye cannot afford to be soft this time around. The big eye knew that if he tried to handle the situation softly, those deckhands who are so blood thirsty may mutiny him. Even his officers can mutiny him which will be far worse considering that they have been working as a team only for them to betray him now that he deserves their loyalty even more. The big eye knew that in the game, nothing is what is seems and therefore nothing can be trusted.

But of course, the KMS was loyal to the big eye; he had never thought of betraying him. His only worry was who he was going to kidnap.

He thought about the number five man of the Eiye Confraternity but he quickly wrote him off. The Airlords can do without him for a considerable length of time. He thought about the number four man but he was always travelling and might not be in school when needed. Something told him that these choices were not good enough for the quick release of their brother. He was trying to avoid the best option, trying to find somebody that would be good enough to replace him. Each time he tried to circumvent the best option, his mind would remind him that his brother is at stake. In the end, he decided to go for the best option.

The best option came to be the number two man of the

Eiye Confraternity. The number two, named Osariemen was a close friend of the KMS in primary school. In secondary school, they were always together, they did things together, they read together, played football together even chase woman together. There was one occasion where they had to sleep with the same girl. Osariemen wooed the girl first. It was so easy that the very day he wooed the girl that very day he slept with her.

When he got tired of her he told his friend about the *generousity* of the girl and that the friend should try his luck. The friend who is now the KMS didn't have to talk much. He was so handsome that the girl fell in love with him immediately. That same day, he slept with her.

So thinking of all the things they had done together, the KMS wasn't at ease with what he was about to do. But what has to be done must be done. He thought again.

Perhaps it was a blessing in disguise that he knew Osariemen only too well. Best of all, he knew Osariemen's girl friend and where she lived. All he had to do was trap him in his girlfriend's place.

That evening he sent some Lords to hang out in Osariemen's girlfriend's place to see if he would be there. But Osariemen didn't go that evening. The next day around 18:30hrs Osariemen was there. All that the KMS needed was four people to carry out the operation. He called the steerer, the hauler and the 2nd shipmate of the deck for the operation. In the Buccaneer's Confraternity, it is the duty of the deck masters to carry out the dirty jobs that needs to be done. But if the deckhands are so adamant to join, then they would be considered. But in this case, there was no need to involve the deckhands. It only took them that is the steerer, hauler, 2nd shipmate and the KMS – about fifteen minutes to get to Osariemen girlfriend's place. They signaled the other lords that they should leave.

Meanwhile, Osariemen was in the room with his girlfriend. The girlfriend was the ferocious type. As a matter of fact, she was a member of the Daughters of Jezebel Confraternity. She was telling Osariemen: "How dare you leave me for a whole week without sex? Don't you know I have been starving? The next time you….."

But Osariemen will not take that shit. Before she would finish her statement, he interrupted her saying: "Cool it off baby, what's the matter with you? Don't you think of anything outside sex? The last time we had sex, you almost drained me out. In the end, I was so wasted. If I continue like that everyday of my life how do you think I would be?"

"Nonsense, why are you a man? Are you not supposed to be doing the job? But I end up doing the job myself and in the end you'll want me to give you milk and cook for you. Never again unless you do a good job."

Osariemen didn't likethe words she used, "Why are you a man?" He was bestial; when he said; "Hey, watch your mouth baby otherwise I will smark your face. What do you mean by you give me milk and cook for me? Don't I give you money to do that?"

"You are not serious, what do you mean you give me money to do that. You give me N1,000.00 at the beginning of a week and you collect N2,000.00 at the end of it. Is that what you mean by give?" She replied him.

This time around he was out of patience. He got up to her and said;

"For the last time I'm warning you, don't dare me otherwise I'm going…." She got up too and faced him. "You coward, do it if you can."

But the way she stood up, the seriousness of her face, the miniskirt she was wearing, that was hugging her ass so closely, the way her boobs was shooting out made her look like a sex bomb. So instead of hitting her like he had promised, he didn't know when he started kissing her. But this was what she had been waiting for and so she returned the kiss passionately.

They were about five minutes in the act when they heard a knock at the door. *Damn it*, the guy cursed, he was already in the spirit.

She didn't like it either. If she had locked the door, she wouldn't have bothered to answer. But then she heard the knock again she said:

"A moment please."

The moment she opened the door, she was surprised to find a .45 automatic pointing at her. Behind the gun was a good looking guy she thought she could seduce to bed on a good day. But when she stared at the eyes of the guy holding the gun and the others behind him, she knew they meant business. The guy holding the gun said: "Go inside."

There wasn't any form of threat in the voice but something told her if she doesn't comply, she would have herself to blame. She was so dumbstruck that she couldn't say a word. She simply obeyed. Her boyfriend, Osariemen was thinking perhaps those were her other boyfriends whom she didn't have the sense to discharge. The thought quickly vanished when he too saw that the .45 automatic was pointed at him. He thought again: *these men must mean business* but he wasn't scared. He looked at them one after the other trying to remember if he knew them somewhere but nothing registered.

The KMS was the one driving the vehicle so he wasn't with them.

One of the boys said: "We want to have a word with you." Although there was no force in the voice, it was cold, cold in such a way that it left no room for doubt that the men will not hesitate to pull the trigger if need be.

"Ok." he said "you can have the word with me here."

"I'm afraid we can't have it here: we need to go outside." the guy holding the gun said.

Osariemen got up to follow them. Something told him they don't mean any harm. But when one of boys asked the girlfriend of Osariemen if she has a scarf, Osariemen wondered what the hell do the people needed a scarf for.

She was trembling when she said "Yes-yes –yes-yes…" more than four times. When she produced the scarf, the guy holding the gun who was the hauler of the deck told the 2nd shipmate to blindfold Osariemen.

Osariemen, who had been so confident all the while lost his balance.

The fear he had never known before crawled up his spine at the mention of blindfold.

His voice was shaking when he asked: "Where are you taking me to?" The hauler replied him; "Don't worry, you'll be safe." he was blindfolded and taken to a car.

Until they reached where they were going, nobody said a word which made Osariemen to be scared shitless.

Because the KMS knew him too well, he had him taken to the hauler's house

The following morning word was sent to the Airlords to release the Buccaneer they are keeping hostage and without any harm unless they want to see their number 2 man killed.

When the Airlords got the message, they quickly arranged a meeting with the Buccaneers for the release of their brother. That same day, the Buccaneer was released to his brothers and when it was confirmed that nothing was wrong with him, and that he was in good health, they in turn released the Airlord in their custody.

Two days later the election kicked off. The election went on smoothly until in the end when it became so obvious that the Buccaneers are going to win. The Airlords, jealous of the fact that they are loosing and the Buccaneers are wining decided to disrupt the whole thing. In their effort to disperse the crowd, a particular Buccaneer stood up to them. Immediately, five men pounced on him. He was beaten mercilessly. It was so severe that he lost conciousness. He was rushed to the hospital that evening. Exams were to start four days later and because of that, the people in charge of the election decided to announce the result of the election. The next day it was announced that Richard the Buccaneer won the position of the president of the Student Union Government with a vote of 2,100, while that of his opponent got a vote of 1,200.

Two days later, a day before exams was to start, the Buccaneer who was rushed to the hospital was discharged so that he could write his exams. But on the condition that he should be coming to the school clinic every day for the dressing of the cuts and wounds on his body.

The deck masters of the Buccaneer's confraternity held an emergency meeting to discuss the event of the week a night to the day of examination. It was concluded that they can't afford to miss their exams. That they can be patient till the day when it would be good enough to make the Airlords pay the price for bloodying their brother. They congratulated themselves on the election they won again. It was 75 % of their power. The KMS asked the house: "Alora me rugged brothers, what if we ask them to pay for the damage and if they pay, then this whole thing can be forgotten."

The Big eye thought for a longtime before he answered. He said

"There won't be any point. Our brother is up now and from the look of things, he would be able to write his exams. I will personally see him to encourage him, as for these high lubbers, the rascals, we are going to show them that hitting a Lord comes with a price."

The house echoed their response. The Big eye continued: "If there's nothing else, I bid you all sail on and success in your exams."

They echoed their response and wished him success in his exams and bade him "sail on!"

And so while the Buccaneers wrote their exams in peace, the Airlords especially the perpetrators of the crime of bloodying a Sealord, were wary. Some of them forfeited their exams because they didn't want to be caught off guard.

What the hell, it is just a first semester exam. Some of them thought.

Chapter 6

The year 1999 was a hell of a year for the different fraternities in the Nigerian higher institutions. When the Neo-Black Movement of Africa, also known as the Black Axe had a fight with the Maphite Confraternity which resulted in the loss of hundreds of lives in Ambrose Alli University, Ekpoma and the fact that Cable News Network (CNN) tagged the institution as the second most violent university in the world, plus the fact that, that same year the Neo Black Movement of Africa also had a fight with the Students' Union Government of Obafemi Awolowo University, Ife whereby the secretary general of the Union was hacked to death on his bed while sleeping and other members of the union were marked for whacking, the Federal Government of Nigeria was forced to leave other problems of the country and tackle the situation of cultism squarely.

The Axemen are renowned freedom fighters. They are known for their violence. In their feverish pursuit of freedom from all kinds of tyranny, they in turn became tyrants' oweing to the power and force they bring down on anybody who stands in their way. They seem to enjoy fighting or better still, they enjoy killing. It is for this reason other fraternities allow them to get away with their little disrespect every now and then because if truth be told, bloodshed is an expensive price to pay for little grievances.

An ultimatum was given by the Federal Government of Nigeria to members of all fraternities that they should publicly renounce whatever cult or fraternity they are affliliated with within the space of one week or the full wrath of the law would be brought down on any person suspected to be a fraternity member.

It was a huge relief for many who had been scared to publicly renounce their fraternities in the county. They knew what would come should they even think of it. There was the case of a medical student who was an Axeman. He was the active type. There's no funtion he doesn't partisipate in. Social gatherings or initiations but overtime, he began to see that, his grades in the different courses were reducing in school. In those courses where he was doing extremely well effortlessly, he was struggling to get an average. He knew the problem. But his real problem was tackling the problem. The issue in itself was simple. It was a problem of decision making. But sometimes simplicity is difficult. Over the years so many people have been ruined that way because they failed to make a standing decision. But this particular medical student was strong willed, he had nerves of steel. When he analyzed the whole thing and discovered that many students have been withdrawn from the university because of their poor performance, he made a risky decision.

Although the decision was tough to make but because as a young blood, he was desirous of fame, power, security and the countless accessories that go with it, he was strong willed. He came to the conclusion that he must renounce. The medical student didn't know he was asking for it when he decided to inform the house of his brave decision to renounce membership.

But in reality, he was a hero. So when he made the decision and informed the house of it, and after he had gone, the number one man of the house reasoned: "*Who does this guy think he is or what does he think of us? Does he think he can just join and leave at his own will? What will others think of us by the time they hear such incredible story?*"

The number two man answered: "It seems he had drank one beer too many. We all know he loves beer; maybe he'll come to his senses and come begging for forgiveness." The number one man responded again: "Nothing of that will happen. We all know that forgiveness is a sin. He has to pay for this insult". The chief butcher didn't like where the conversation was heading. He quickly said; "Let's hit him a little. Enough to sustain a long time wound but not a fatal one." The number one man said "Are you kidding me? Tomorrow when he is drinking beer, he would be bragging to his friends that he did this and did that and got away scot free. Chief butcher, you are to take with you three Axemen tomorrow and night the infidel".

The next day. The medical student was coming from college when four men rounded him up and slit his throat. It was a lesson for the rest.

And so when the Federal Government proposed a one week grace for all fraternity members to renounce, it was a welcom idea. During that week, thousands publicly renounced. In Ambrose Alli University alone, over a thousand fraternity members renounced. Most of them were from the Maphite, Axemen, Eiye and Vikings Confraternity.

The few that renounced in the Buccaneer and Pyrate Confraternity were the laggers in the confraternity, they were the few who lacked proper orientation of what the fraternity stands for. In all these, a lot of guns from pump action, double barrel, pistol and locally made guns plus other weapons like battle axe, cutlass, and knives of different sizes were given up by the students. These weapons were gathered and burned. The next stage was for them to go to churches and confess. A greater number were Catholics.

Although in the Catholic Church confessions is done one person at a time but because of the massive turn out of cultists, the Catholic Church in Ekopma, Mary the Queen Catholic Church, decided to do a group confession and absolving.

But for those especially the Buccaneers and Pyrates who were married to the game, who had no intentions of divorcing the bitch, because the bitch was the sweetest thing to them, had no choice but to remain faithful till the end. They were the rarest of men who knew what bravery and ruggedity meant. The Buccaneers Confraternity even composed a sea song to the effect that Obasanjo the president at the time was a lubber and had no right to give them orders. But a particular fratman named Edison was really troubled. He had committed so many atrocities that killing and raping were the least of them. When he heard that the priest of the Catholic Church were absolving members of different fraternities from their sins, he couldn't believe it. In his opinion, nobody had such powers. Although he was a Catholic he couldn't remember the last time he went to church let alone read the Bible or receive communion. But he was firm in his belief that God cannot grant such a power to any person or organization be it a church or whatever.

He was an Axeman, an ex chief butcher, so the atrocity he had committed was haunting him. He kept seeing the ghosts of people he had killed. He couldn't live with himself anymore. Already, he had spent nine years in school doing a course of four years. Worse still, he was sure as Christ was sure of Himself as God that there was no hope of him graduating that year. Finally, frustrated with himself and life, he started crying. He knew he needed help but where to get it was the problem. While he was crying, a small voice inside of him kept repeating to him, "Go for confession" over and over again.

Rev. Father Michael Okiro, is one of those Priest that has true sympathy for sinners. Whenever those for confession are absolved by him, they felt like angels. The weight they have been carrying about just disappears automatically. But there are many who question the authority of the church to forgive sins. Although Edison was one of them, he decided to go and see if he could get help. This time around, the number of students coming out for confession had reduced to such that individual confession was now possible. He was the next in line. The person confessing before Edison seemed to be taking forever to come out. Edison was wondering if the person's sins was as worse as his. Finally the guy came out and it was his turn.

Once more, he said an act of contrition as he was approaching the confessional: *"Bless me father, for I have sinned, it's been seven years since my last confession; since then I have sinned through my thoughts, words, deeds and omission and I accuse myself of the following sins:*

I belong to a fraternity called the Neo-Black Movement of Africa aka Black Axe.

I plotted the death of a fellow member so that I can become the head of the fraternity.

I arranged with others of my fraternity to rob my friend's parents but in the process the dad was shot dead.

I have killed so many I cannot count.

I arranged with others to have my sister's friend raped.

I find it difficuit to believe in the teachings of the church.

I don't believe in God anymore…"

At this, the priest, Father Mike cut him off. He asked; *"Then why did you come for confession?"* Edison replied him; *"Father, I'm dying. I see ghosts every now and then. Inside of me is like hell. I know I need help but I don't know where to get it from but something kept repeating inside me 'go for confession' again and again, that is why I came."*

The father pitied him. He saw how hopeless he was. He said; *"This is what you'll do. You'll wait for me till I'm through with the confession: your case is special. It is a great sin not to believe in God. Have you been baptized?"*

"Yes Father" Edison Replied.

"Good, you just wait, ok?"

"Ok father." Edison replied.

After he was through with the confession he came to

Edison and asked:

"*Son what is your name?*"

"*Edison.*"

"*Mr. Edison, I'm happy you've made the right choice; it is not a mistake that you are here. God wants you to be saved. What will you be doing tomorrow?*"

"*Nothing Father.*" Edison replied.

"*Ok, I want you to come tomorrow. What we'll be discussing will take time. It is after six o'clock now and I'm exhausted from hearing confessions, can you come tomorrow around 10:00hrs?*"

Edison had no choice, he said; "*Yes.*"

The day in question happened to be a nice day especially for the Rev. Father who had asked Edison to come around 10:00hrs. He woke up that morning feeling good. He said his prayers, took his bath, and celebrated a mass for those faithful who'd rather miss a day's food than to miss the Holy Communion. After that he ate his breakfast and waited for his guest. His kingsize pleasure was to see sinners saved. It was 30 minitues before Edison would arrive. He decided to pray his rosary while waiting for Edison.

When Edison arrived he was dressed in casual white T-shirt and a black jeans trouser and a leather black sandal. He was looking sobar. In his mind he was like, – *will anything good come out of this?* Still he went straight to the parish house, knocked and waited.

He was going to knock the second time when he heard the door slip open. Fortunately, it was Father Mike.

Father Mike ushered him in, made him sit on a sofa. He went to the fridge and brought out two bottles of Coka-cola drink. He gave one to Edison and opened one for himself.

He sat on a leather sofa opposite Edison. The lounge was 16m by 20m wide with marble tiles for a floor finish and a POP for the ceiling.

A crucifix hung on one side of the wall, the picture of Mary was hung on the opposite side of it. A framed picture of St. Augustine and his mother were also hung on one side of the wall. A large frame of the Lord's Supper adorned the last side of the wall.

Edison couldn't help but think that *these Reverened Fathers are really enjoying.* For a second, the thought flashed across his mind that maybe he should become a Rev. Father. But the thought vanished immeditely. He loved women far too much to make a good priest. While coming to the Parish house, he couldn't help but notice that the least car parked in the parking lot was a Benz clk 2007 model. He looked at the priest again. The priest was looking so fresh and hand-some. He thought for the one thousandth time again. What is it that drives a man to make him want to do this kind of job? Giving up the sweet pleasure of sex and the comfort of a beautiful, sexy, romantic and understanding wife. What could be sweeter than to have a good and understanding wife who welcomes you with a hug as you come from work, prepares that delicious meal that makes the man go haywire with love, makes sure that the house is neat and tidy, prepares the bathroom for him, ensures that his clothes are clean, care for him to the extent that the man begins to think he is a child all over again? Of course every man deserves such. The world is so hard that without the comfort of a woman a person might go crasy. What about the beauty of seeing your kids grow up? Seeing them pass from one stage to the other. Correcting them when they do wrong even hitting them when it is absolutely necessary. Oh that joy of hearing your kids say *Daddy good morning, daddy welcome.* How those men who are married without kids crave to hear such. With all these beauties, it is difficult to believe that a person will give these things up to be a celibate. If these people choose to be celibate, then luxury houses and cars are but a small consolation for them. For what good are houses and cars to any person without a person of his blood to enjoy it with?

Father Mike interrupted his thoughts by saying: "Son, the Catholic faith is one of the greatest controversies in the world. It takes the grace of God to truly understand the faith. But first we are going to talk about God. Why is it so difficult for you to believe in God?"

Edison thought about it for a moment then replied. "I think that is the problem. I mean why should I believe in God? The way most religions have put him is like you have to appease Him with gifts, money, even flatter Him with praise so as to gain favour from Him or buy off his divine wrath. The problem with this is that, while it favours the rich, it disfavours the poor because they don't have the money to propitiate him. How can such a God be called a good God.

"Looking at it more closely, it is like God is the invention of the white man to keep the poor and black at bay from revolting against them.

Again, looking at how God was painted in the Old Testament, one cannot help but be terrified of such a God. Imagine that for the sin of one man, generations after generations will suffer the consequences.

The story of Pharaoh is another tale to wonder at. This

tale proves that God takes delight in showing off. Ok, let's say that Pharaoh was wrong by taking the Israelites captive for over 400 years, does that justifies the act of God by sending the land of Egypt plagues? Worse still, the first born of every family was whacked. Of course even though the majority of Egyptians like the idea of having the Israelites captive in their land, there are those who felt that what Pharaoh was doing was wrong but for fear that if they let know their opinion, they might be whacked, they decided not to voice out their opinion. The Bible didn't make mention of those families that only had a child and were also whacked or the families that had just given birth to their first child but because of the stubborness of Pharoah, their children were also whacked. And the same Bible told us that God is just. The irony of it is that in that same book of the Bible, Genesis, we were told that Abraham pleaded with God and asked that if there are as few as ten righteous people in the land of Sodom and Gomorrah, will God not spare the land; and we were told that God promised not to destroy the land if there are as few as ten righteous people in the land. With these incidents one cannot help but wonder if the God who had the first born in the land of Egypt whacked and the God who promised to spare the people of Sodom and Gomorrah if ten righteous people can be found among them, is one and the same God."

All the while, Father Mike was nodding his head as if to say Edison was justified in not believing in God.

Edison continued: "You know father, this Bible thing is fishy, and it looks like a scam. I have been thinking about this for a long time. I still think the Bible is an idea of the white man to keep people under subjection. Let's look at the issue of God again. Don't you think that God discriminates, huh? Why would He prefer the Israelites over other tribes or nations? In my opinion, it is either God saw that he has fucked up and He wanted others to know that He is still in control by making Himself their God to defend and bless them or the white men didn't arrange the story well.

"Off course, over time people no longer regarded God anymore. They didn't see any reason to worship Him because He had made a mess of everything."

One great asset of Father Mike is listening. He wanted Edison to air out his grief so that he can know what to do to help him. But at the mention of "God has fucked up", he quickly made the sign of the cross on himself and when Edison made mention of God had made a mess of everything, the priest looked at Edison with a cold look that would have scared the hell out of the most wretched of sinners. Although he did it unintentionally, in his opinion, it was the devil that was talking. But he didn't interrupt him and so Edison continued.

"Father, are you listening? Like I said before" Edison continued: "The Bible is fishy. When the white men saw that people were too headstrong, that the Bible was not terrifying enough to bring people under their subjection, they decided to introduce something new. Although at that time, it was written in the Bible that a saviour called Emmanuel would come and when finally he came, people still didn't believe in his message, but the white men took advantage of his coming. His message was hijacked and the concept of hell fire was introduced. Now what I don't understand is how can

God who loves us so much to the extent of sacrifishing his only begotten son (*mind you according to what they wrote to prove to us that He really cares and loves us,*) now create something like hell fire where people will burn for all eternity if they refuse to love Him. The thing is: why should God threaten us with hell fire at all? Is it necessary that we should love Him? In my opinion, God is greater than this. By the time the love is returned forcefully, it becomes null and void. We now love Him because we want something in return."

This time the Reverend interrupted him: "No, that is not true" He was going to say more but he noticed that Edison was not through with what he had to say. So he waited for Edison to continue. Edison continued:

"The more I read the New Testament, the more I find out that something is not right with the way it was narrated, what I think is, in the white man's feverish pursuit of bringing the world under subjection, he forgot or failed to make the stories support each other. One of the many instances the Bible failed to collaborate with each other is the narration of the crucifixion of Jesus Christ. While Matthew and Mark believe that the two bandits crucified with Christ insulted Christ, Luke believed that only one of the bandits did so and the other rebuked him for doing so and asked Christ to remember him when He gets to His kingdom of which Jesus replied him saying: *I promise you that today you will be in paradise with me.*

So you see Father, the problem here is that the same Bible told us that the words written in it are inspired by the Holy Spirit. The Holy Spirit, the author of truth as I know, cannot contradict Himself"

The priest interrupted him again: "Let me get something straight, it is not as if you do not believe in God, but in the way God has been presented to you, right?" A smile flashed across Edison's face when he said: "Something like that but there are still reasons why I believe the issue of God is a scam."

"Can you tell me about these reasons?" the Father asked.

"I would rather rest my case here Father" Edison replied him.

Father Mike sighed. He relaxed back in his chair. In the 15 years he has been a priest he had never doubted God or his faith in God but with what Edison has said so far he couldn't help but freely think that maybe perhaps the idea of God is a scam. He realized that what Edison had been trying to point out but didn't say out loud was that God is wicked if really He is as portrayed by the Bible. In that particular moment Father Mike doubted his Catholic faith. But he quickly recovered. He had taken a vow, he must not abandon God. He looked at Edison again and wondered if maybe he was an agent of the Freemasons. Meanwhile, Edison was waiting for him.

"My son" Father Mike began, "I have come across many who seem to think the way you do that God is not just or worse He does not exist. But the fact that you and millions of your type think so does not underwhelm the fact that God exists and not just that, He is a just God. Let me tell you a story. Once upon a time, there lived a certain man of God, he was so troubled about the nature of God, that he wanted to know Him inside out. Most times in order to contemplate the person of God, he secludes himself from the crowd to a place of solitude to mediatate about God. He kept doing this over and over again troubling himself unnecessarily. One day, he decided to go to the bank of the sea to meditate. As he was meditating, he noticed a young boy doing something odd which if truth be told it was a foolish act. This young boy dug a small hole some few steps away from the sea. With a spoon in his hand, he would go to the sea, collect water with the table spoon, and go to hole he had dug and pour the water into it. At first, this man of God thought the boy was playing but when it became obvious that the young boy was serious with his idea of transferring the sea into the small hole he had dug, this man of God felt pity for the young boy. He went to the young boy and asked: *"Young boy, what do you think you are doing?"* The young boy replied, *"I want to transfer this large sea of water (he pointed to the sea) "into this hole I have dug."*

The man of God laughed. He said: *"Young boy that is a foolish idea, don't waste your time trying to do that, it can never be accomplished. Go find something better to do with your time."*

But the young boy smiled and said: *"This small hole I have dug can be likened to the human brain and the large sea, God and just like the small hole cannot contain the ocean so also your little brain cannot comprehend God. The human brain can never comprehend God so don't waste your time trying to comprehend God."*

After he said that, the young boy vanished. Without doubt, the young boy was Divine and the man of God is the person of Saint Augustine. It is a true story. But you see, it is not in our place to tell God what He is to do with His creatures. That is the reason He is God. There are so many things going on at the same time; that is why sometimes it is difficult to understand why certain things happen. God who is infinitely good, allows certain things to happen for a greater good. Of course as God, He does not need our permission to act. You know, it grieves my heart when I see people not appreciating God. Even some of the disabled and the sick appreciatiate God. What now is the reason why the healthy and those without any form of physical disability not appreciate God? You wake up everyday physically healthy without even knowing what might have transpired in the night while you were deep in sleep, is it not enough to say *thank you father.* If you think you are going to make me give you reasons why you should love and appreciate God, you've got another think coming. If you are wise, if you open your eyes wide enough then without doubt you'll find that you'll need to hire a taxi to take you to the end of list of the reasons you need to love and appreciate God. You see, certain people are blaming God today because God didn't judge Satan justly. They claim that God is not just. That He forgives us over and over again when we sin, yet refuses to forgive Satan, they say unlike us men, God was too harsh on Satan. That why couldn't He forgive Satan for once that Satan sinned."

Edison was stunned. He couldn't believe that men would dare hold grudge against God. At least not on the issue of Satan who has caused so much havoc in the world. From the way Edison was staring, Father Mike knew what was running in his mind. He only said:

"You would think that men are wise. For the most foolish of reasons they would betray whoever they want to betray even God. But what I want to point out to you is that God loves you so much. You see He did not hesitate to cast out

Satan and all those angels who took side with him out of His Kingdom just because of a lack of respect from Satan. But you and I have been so privileged if we have a contrite heart, no matter the kind of sin, God will forgive us. A privilege He didn't grant Satan his most beautiful angel. Like I said to you before. You'll need to hire a cab that will take you to the end of the list of reasons I can give though be sure the cab can not get to the end of that list."

Edison smiled at the thought of it. His thinking was: *what possible reasons can Father Mike give that will make him hire a cab.* He said: "Father Mike, I do not hold a grudge against God but only in the way He was presented in the Bible. He is portrayed as somebody who shares the same blood with Satan."

"Trust me" Father Mike said "God can be ferocious with his enemies if it is absolutely necessary. That is the side of Him you do not want to know. If He really wants to punish you, believe me, going to hell will be just like going to Disneyland. It will be the least of your problems."

"Excuse me Father," Edison interrupted "Are you trying to tell me that going to hell fire is more or less like a favour from God?"

"All I'm trying to say is don't be like the Freemasons who worship Satan and in the process hold a grudge against God like they can kill God or win in the fight. These people don't know what they have coming. By the time it hits them, hell fire will be the least of their problems."

Edison couldn't help it. He became interested in the Freemasons. The idea seemed to appeal to him that anybody would think of holding grudge against God, he said: "Father, can you tell me about the Freemasons?"

The father sighed, "I can never tell you enough, these people are very secretive and very powerful. Like I said, I can never tell you enough."

"Just tell me the little you can Father. " Edison pleaded.

"Hmm, where will I start from?" Father Mike began "The Freemasons is a secret society of an international order, I can't really tell about their origin but they have been existing way back before America was found. Matter of fact, they are the founding fathers of America. Like I told you before, they are doing Satan's bid. They say God was unjust when He decided the fate of Satan. Of course, they are worshippers of Satan and they are standing up for him to rebel against God. As a result, they have associated themselves with anything that is against God or even rebellious. For instance, the number 13 is one of their symbols. You may be wondering why 13, but as you will see, the first time 13 occured in the Bible was as a result of a rebellious act, it first appeared in genesis 14:4 where we read *Twelve years they served Chedornomer, and the thirteenth years they REBELLED*. Hence every occurrence of the number 13 stands in connection with rebellion, apostasy, defection, disintegration corruption and revolution. Of course you'll agree with me that America was founded by a rebellious act torwards England. Another number they associate themselves with is the number 33. You may be wondering why 33 again. But then Anti-Christ was mentioned 33 times in the Old Testament and 13 times in the New Testament. Are you seeing the significance of these numbers?"

"Yes Father" Edison replied. Mike continued:

"There is another symbol which they use. Perhaps it

should be called logo or emblem. It is a pyramid with a eye in the middle on a two- dimensional plat form, it looks like a triangle, have you seen anything of this sort anywhere?"

"I can't say." Edison replied.

"Think again, perhaps something foreign."

"Have you seen the American dollar?"

"Yes Father and there is something like a triangle on it."

"Good, that is a logo of the Freemason. They control practically everything in America, just name it. Even on their great seal, almost everything is 13 in number. Since they are the bedrock of everything in American, it is no wonder that almost all the presidents that had ruled America are masons or puppets of Freemasonry. Do you know that part in the Bible that talks about a new world order?" Although Edison hardly reads the scripture but he could remember from way back when he was so ardent about God's ways such things as new world order but he didn't concern himself with that. After all it will not happen in his time. Hearing the father bring the topic again made him apprehensive. He simply said "Yes."

Ok, on that same dollar bill where the top of the pyramid was detached from the rest of the pyramid with the all Seeing Eye, there is this Latin word 'Novus Ordo Seclorum' which also means bringing in the new order. But before this there must be chaos in the world and when it is settled and a new order is brought in, they the Freemasons would be the world leaders. Does this tell you anything?"

Edison looked like he was going to shit in his pants, he had this worrisome look on his face. He said:

"Father you know, when Nostradamus predicted the

bombing of the world Trade Centre, he also said that it would ignite a war which would be more devastating than the others. But I was so happy when it didn't result to third world war.

"Does this mean that there is going to be a Third World War? The thought of it sickens me."

"In my opinion yeah. And in a way the war is already going on and by the time the war subsides it will be the illuminists in behalf of Anti-Christ that would be ruling the world. Mind you the world trade centre was not the doing of the Muslims, the Freemason had that operation planned out decades ago before the incident." Edison was so shocked that his mouth refused to close, if not that he was breathing one would have thought he was a fine piece of art work.

"Damn, I can't believe this shit I'm hearing."

"Yes, shit happens." the Father said.

"All along I've been thinking the Muslims were behind that hit. You mean to tell me Father that the Freemanson were behind that hit?"

"Their aim was to cause a world war so that by the time it is over they would take control over the world. Although they have achieved that through the internet it remains to be seen physically." "Wait a minute Father, the eye in their emblem, what does it stand for?"

"Where have you been all these while? You are so blind. Stephen Wonder sees more than you do. You need to step out of that darkness. You mean to tell me you don't know any of these? Of course the eye is the all seeing eye of the Horus. Horus as you know is one of the Egyptian gods. And the Egyptian then were practicing a false religion of magic.

The eye simply represents a demonic eye. The Freemans are telling the world that no one escapes the magical reaches of their eye: in other words they see everything and they know everything. Their pride is that they have always existed since the time of the first world power till now and as the Bible told us, Egypt was the first world power that brought civilization to mankind. Although no one truly knows their origin, there are some Freemasons who will slice your throat if you tell them to their face they are from Egypt.

"Some sources hinted that they started since the time of King Solomon. Precisely when King Solomon had the magnificent temple built. They had their name from the word 'Mason'. Mason in the Middle Ages were stone builders. Over time they became so skilled in the art that they decided to form an organization. The fundamental rule was that they would be freelance stone builders not subject to government or anybody. It was for this reason they decided to call themselves Freemasons. Because it was a trade that was a booming, they decided to keep the skills of the craft a secret. It was also this reason they became a secret society so that anybody who wishes to dabble in the trade and excel will have to join their society. They are a mobile fraternity of skilled workers, moving from town to town building massive castle, cathedrals and bridges. In time they became the architects as well as the masons. In the early 17th century, Scottish masons developed special handshake and password which soon spread around all the lodges. Lodges are secret places where masons hold their meetings."

"Are these meetings secret and are there any rituals involved?" Edison asked.

"Of course, many even believed that with their secrecy, symbolism and rituals, certain hermetic truth was handed down from acient civilization. They became so powerful that people from other professions lobbied to become members of the society to gain power and influnce and political connections. Oddly enough, the society became known for their intellectual ability. But the problem with knowledge is, it makes one a deist or worse an atheist and the Freemasons were no exception. As if that was not enough, they started to dabble in occult practices. As with all secrets, the Freemason eventually were known for their Atheistic beliefs. Immediately, the Holy Catholic Church banned anybody associated with Freemasonry from the church. That was the beginning of their beef with the Catholic Church. By the end of the 18th century, the stigma attached to Freemasonry by clerical and civil authorities had taken hold. Pope Clemenx XII issued his papal bull in Eminenti banning Freemasonry and forbidding lodge membership for Catholics. In other words no Catholic was to be a Freemason. Many other popes did the same thing using the most vitriolic language possible to condemn freemasonry but it was Pope Pious IX that outdid his papal predecessors, he condemned freemasonry in six seperate papal bulls between 1846 and 1873."

"What was their reaction to this?"

"Of course, they went underground. But most of them were practicing Catholics. One thing that can be said about them is that they are mercurial. They can assume anything just to infiltrate an organization. Of course, they've infiltrated major religions in the world including Islam and Christianity. In most of the orthodox churches, they are the heads but their greatest challenge is to bring down the Catholic Church."

Edison was amazed again that anybody would think of such. He asked: "Is the church aware of this?"

"Of course the Pope is aware but the problem is these people are fellow Catholics like you and I. Infact, some of them are Priests. Worse still, even the cardinals close to the pope are Freemasons but you can't know because they celebrate mass with such fervour you would think they are already saints. They are already promoting such ideas like the crucifix should be removed from the church and women should start celebrating Mass and such like fooleries. They are trying to use the age old tactics of divide and conquer. They are trying to promote doctrines contrary to the teachings of the church that would cause disunity and therefore division."

"It seems the Catholic Church is deep down in shit" Edison said "How are we going to win this war when we don't know whom to fight?"

"Yeah, it is more of a spiritual war and our Lord Jesus Christ and His angels will do the fighting while we stand back and watch like in the case of Fatima. Do you still remember that story?"

"Yeah, I know the blessed Mary appeared to three little children and asked them to make sacrifices to reduce the number of souls that go to hell."

"Good, that aside, do you know another reason why the apparition took place in Portugal?"

"No Father."

"Ok, what most people don't know is that prior to the

apparition in 1917 in Portugal, the Freemasons in 1910 took power in Portugal with a provision government by force of arms. The first act of this government on October 8, 1910 was so suppress all religious congregations and to expel the Jesuits. A few days later, they abolished the religious oath in the court system and then on the 25th, they abolished the oath to defend the immaculate conception of the Blessed Virgin Mary in the schools. In the same month, they decreed that all religious holidays were to be days of work. On November 3, 1910, divorce was legalized for the first time in Portugal. On Christmas Day in 1910 marriage was declared to be a purely civil contract and on the 31st of December 1910, the priests and nuns who were allowed to remain in Portugal were not allowed to wear religious dress or habits on pain of imprisonment. On April 20, 1911, church buildings were confisicated and were used as barracks, stables and government building, convents and monasteries became jails and offices for the Government.

"Magalhaes Lima, grand master of the Portuguese Freemasonry declared that within a few years no one would want to be a priest. Another Freemason, Afonso Casta declared that the new law of separation of church and state would end the Catholic Church in two generations. In other words the dogma of faith would be lost forever"

"Wow! This is interesting. What now happened after that? Edsion asked. The Father paused for a while then said:

"I've been talking for a long time now. Don't you think you should buy me a bottle of beer to wet the throat?"

"Ah father, do you drink beer?"

"Why not, beer is good for the body so long as it is not

too much."

"I've been meaning to ask this question. When exactly does beer become too much? I know of people who drink as many as six bottles of beer and they feel like they have not drank anything. For such people would you say six bottles is too much?"

"I guess that's a question for doctors not Priests. Let's get back to our previous discussion. But you said you know the story." Not how it affected the Freemasons"

"Damn, do I have to go through this? Look young man you owe me a bottle of beer."

"Don't worry Father I'll buy you six"

The father's smile was from ear to ear when he asked.

"Are you for real?"

"Sure as I breathe, Father." "Ok, let's make it seven bottles to make it divine."

With the promise of seven bottles of beer, Father was gingered. He continued:

"As you know, the angel prepared the children. Lucia, Jacinta and Francisco in 1916 for a visit from our lady. The angel appeared to them three times before our Lady now came in May. The children were so excited that they couldn't keep it to themselves. Soon what was supposed to be a secret was made known to their parents. Their parents were so happy that they told their friends. Their friends also told their friends everybody wanted to be connected to it as if it is an assurance of salvation. In June, our Lady appeared again, July she appeared. This time around, everybody knew of the Apparition of the Blessed Virgin Mary. But in August the children were not to be found."

The Mayor of Villa Nova de Ourem which emcompasses Fatima was Arthur Santos. He was a renowned Freemason. Prior to his being a mayor, he had been publishing a newspaper called *Ouriense,* which attacked the monarchy of the church in the small towns of Ourem and Fatima. He was elected to the Masonic lodge of liera and later founded his own lodge in Ourem-Fatima. Due to his loyalty to the Freemasons, he was elected Mayor at the age of 26 when the Freemasons took power in Portugal." The father paused then continued: "The Mayor, Arthur Santos was already furious, he called the three children to his office on August 11, 1917 but Ti Mario, the father of Jacinta and Francisco would not take them, and instead, he went himself. Lucia the eldest of the three children and her father, Antonio went with Ti Mario. In the meeting, the Major threatened Lucia with death and questioned Antonio and Ti Mario. Although Antnio did not yet believe in the apparitions but Ti Mario did so and said so. On August 13, 1917, the Mayor devised a plan. On that same day, some of the faithful gathered; about five thousand of them to witness the apparition of the Blessed Virgin Mary. Arthur Santos convincing the parents of the children that he too was interested in seeing our Blessed Mother asked the parents to bring the children so that they can go in his carriage to see and believe like St. Thomas. When the children arrived, they were shocked. This wasn't the arrangement. But Ti Mario reassured them. He said: "Senhor Administrator wants to take you to the Cova in his carriage. Lucia said: *We'll prefer to walk.* The administrator Arthur Santos quickly cut in: Well, *just this once you can ride with me. We must see father Ferreira before you go to cova da Iria so come with me.* They went fast to the parish church to see the priest but this was a ploy to go away from the little village called Cova in which the blessed virgin was to appear, and towards Ouriem where he resides. After a pretence with the priest the Mayor thrust the children into the cart and left Ti Mario standing in the dust looking furious. Meanwhile, large crowd was waiting at Cova de Iria to witness an apparition of the Blessed Virgin Mary. While they were waiting a message was brought that the three children had been kidnapped by the Mayor. They all were enraged. They said: *since the Mayor has kidnapped the children, let's all go to his office and storm it down let's storm the city. They cannot stop all of us, they cannot do this to little children.* But almost at the same time, a sudden flash of lightening and thunder stopped the shouting of the crowds, everyone spread away from the tree, then lightning busted out upon the Cova. *We will be killed without the children a woman shouted.* Then quietly a little cloud, very delicate, very white, stopped for a few moments over the tree and then rose in the air and disappeared. With this the crowd was excited, their faces reflected the colours of the rainbow: pink, red, blue. The tress seemed to be made not of leaves but of flowers, they seemed to be laden with flowers. The ground and their clothes shone brighty with different colours. Even the lanterns fixed to the tree look like gold. As the sign disappeared, all the people set out for Fatima shouting against the Mayor, even against the priest and anyone who they thought had anything to do with the imprisonment of the children.

"But the Mayor, in order to avoid the crowd took the children to his own house. In his house, he threatened them with death if they refuse to tell him the secrets the blessed

Virgin has been telling them. The threat had no effect on them. The Mayor thought maybe he wasn't convincing enough. He took them to a place where a big pot of oil was boiling and threatened he was going to put them one by one into the oil should they refuse to tell him the secrets the Blessed virgin has been telling them. Still nothing registered. He became exasperated. He threatened again saying: *Ok, no more fooling arrround you brats. You're going to tell me the secret or you'll never see your parents again. So what was it she told you?* Jacinta who had earlier asked the blessed Mary if she can go with her to heaven was the first to come out for her to be thrown into the boiling oil. In her mind the earlier she leaves this world, the quicker, then she can live the rest of her life with the blessed Virgin, her blessed mother. When the blessed Virgin appeared to them, she asked them if they are willing to make sacrifices for the conversion of sinners and they said yes, she told them again that they were going to suffer many things but she would always be with them. So when the issue of boiling oil came, they were more than willing to scarifice their lives for the conversion of sinners. Immediately she offered to go to her death, Francisco the least of the children just six years old followed her sister and then Lucia their cousin. When the Mayor saw that they were willing to die, he gave up. On the third day of their imprisonment, which was the feast of Assumption of the Blessed Virgin Mary and like Christ rose up from the dead the third day, the children were set free. The Mayor personally took them to their Parish and dropped them. It was after the close of Mass the parishioners including the father of Jacinta and Francisco saw the children.

They were all filled with joy at the sight of the three children. On the 20th of August the same month the children were imprisoned, our Lady appeared to them again and bid them to continue to say their rosaries. Lucia was even bold enough to ask if she would perform a miracle for all to see and she said: *Yes but it will be in October, and if you have not been imprisoned the miracle would have been greater.* In September she appeard and in October as she had promised she appeared again. But on that particular day, while the people were gathered waiting, rain fell heavily and soaked them. No sooner had the rain stopped when the Blessed Virgin appeared. She brought with her her chaste spouse St. Joseph who was carrying the infant Jesus in his hand. The sun that looked like it wasn't ready to shine again for that day suddenly glowed. Matter of fact it was golden. All of a sudden it dropped. The people were so terrified they thought it was going to drop on them. People were already running but just as it was about to land on them, it hanged again. It rolled from one place to the other. One would have thought that with the heat of the sun they would have been fried but instead they enjoyed the warmth that came from it and in no time their clothes were dried. When all their clothes were dried, the sun went back to its former position. As the Holy family: Jesus, Mary and Joseph were about to leave. The infant Jesus blessed the crowd and they followed an eastern direction back to where they came from. Till this day Portuguese celebrates August 13th as one of the great feast days of Fatima."

"Why August 13th? After all, she appeared from May to October and even performed a miracle on October for all to see. In my opinion, October 13th should be celebrated not August 13th." Edison said. The people of Fatima chose August 13th because that was the day the Blessed Mary fought and defeated the Freemasons. That was the day she performed a miracle even though the children were not there in Cova de Iria. Five thousand people saw the little cloud, the lightning, the rainbow of colours, it was the day she started her war with the anti-catholic government of Portugal. She even promised that even though the catholic faith would be lost in other parts of the world, it would be preserved in Portugal till the coming of her son Jesus Christ."

The father paused then continued, "The following year, the Mayor was fired and the diocese was restored. In 1921, the communist tried to take over the government but by 1926 Salazar took power and restored all the church property and rights."

"It seems they were defeated". Edison said.

"Although, they lost that particular battle, they have been wining others." The Father pointed out. "Others like which father?" Edison asked.

"Because you are so blind that the bat sees more than you, I doubt if you've heard of the word 'illuminati'?"

"Why not!" Edison exclaimed. "Is it not a name of a soap or is it cream? Well, between the two." Father Mike laughed. He said; "You are really dumb. Maybe that explains why you've been in school for so many years. But this is an irony. One would have thought that your job in school is to read. What do you do with your time any way?"

"Well, you heard my confession yesterday. Those are some of the things I do with my time. Father if truth be told, in the street I grew up from reading is for..."

"For who?" father Mike asked. 'Well it doesn't matter." Edison replied. Edison didn't want to give the father the impression that he is a suckers. Father Mike gave him that look of his again. A look that made Edison's spine crawl up with fear. Edison was wondering if Father Mike was an Assassin. He has heard rumours that certain fathers in Europe take jobs of assassination to make ends meet. Father Mike broke his line of thought by saying; "That is your funeral." as if he knew what Edison was thinking.

"Anyway," the father continued; "the Illuminati, unlike the Freemasons had a different objective. The real Freemasons are those who believe in nature, reason and progress that is they believe that if man takes the time to reason things out with nature guiding him, Man will ultimately make progress. In other words, they would not need any person like God to save them. This is the true philosophy of the Masons. Where man can evolve himself into a God, living eternally happy forever and shaping nature to his wishes. There were also those involved in occultic practices. Some even believed in Jesus Christ. It became a matter of secrets within secrets like treachery within treachery. Eventually, sects began to split out. The Preure du Sion, one of the sects that broke out held that Jesus Christ had a blood lineage that is even preserved till date. If you've watched the Da Vinci code or even read the novel you will know what I'm talking about."

"I have watched the film, Father."

"Ok, at least you have an idea of what I'm saying. So in 1776, a new sect was founded: the ORDER OF THE ILUMINATI. Their mission was to enlighten the world.

This was professor Weishaupt's idea. He had a vision of a world free of the constraints of government and the crushes of all kinds of religions particularly the Catholic faith. They encouraged their members to strive for perfection both interiorly and exteriorly. And that they through their deeds would be the light of the world. Don't forget, all I've been trying to tell you is that while they must have lost in Fatima at Portugal, they have won in other places. Aside the American government, the CIA, FBI, the police, they have hijacked the film and music industry among others. It is through film and music that they propagate their message. These days' actors and actress sell their souls in order to get fame and wealth. Half of the famous people you see in the media today are being controlled by the Illuminati or Freemason. It is not clear which infiltrated which but somewhere along the line objectives of each kindda merged."

"Damn!" Edison exclaimed "I like Jay-Z. He's one of my favourite rappers." If he is one of your favourite rappers, how come you" have not seen him make that symbol of triangle with his hands and sometimes he does it with one of his eyes in the middle. Does that not tell you anything?"

"Holy shit!" Edison exclaimed again but the father quickly rebuked him. He scolded him that such fowl languge was venial sins and if it becomes too much, it will result to mortal sin.

Edison fronted a face of remorsefulness. When the father saw that, he was relieved that at least he was penitent. Edison continued: "I have been seeing that sign in some of his videos; I didn't know it meant something, I thought it was just one of those things that rappers do. But how do you know these things Father?" I would have thought as a priest you are not to concern yourself with the secular world."

"Yeah, just like the Freemasons or Illuminati, we also have our eyes to see."

"I don't know how to put it Father, but there is something mystifying about the Catholic faith; sometimes when I try to analyze the Catholic faith, I always end up believing that the Catholic church is the anti- Christ: there are so many things the Catholic Church does that is contrary to the Bible, yet there is so much truth in what they preach. Please Father can you enlighten me about the teaching of the church as regards the Bible?"

"Ahh! The Catholic Church, has been in so many dangers since the time Christ founded it. Aside the Freemasons and Illuminatis, there are other forces trying to bring it down. There's one quote I relish so much. It was said by St .Augustine. No doubt St. Augustine is one of the greatest theologians the world has ever known. He said "I would not believe the Gospel itself if the authority of the Catholic Church did not move me to do so." If only you know the comfort I derive from this quote. The Catholic Church was founded by Jesus Christ himself, the author of truth. It is really an irony when people accuse the church of preaching foreign messages not in the Bible, or practices idolatry. But let's look at it carefully, how did the Bible come about? Who compiled the Bible? What served as the final authority for Christians before the Bible was compiled? These are some of the questions you should ask yourself."

"I know the Catholic Church is the first church and by way of logic, it must have been founded by Christ, but I think somewhere down the line, the church deviated from the truth written in the Bible." Edison said.

"The first misconception I want you to get right is that the Bible did not produce the Church, rather it is the Church that produced the Bible. Matter of fact, it was the church that wrote the Bible under the inspiration of the Holy Spirit. The Israelites as the Old Testament church or pre-Catholics and the early Catholics as the New Testament church. In the pages of the New Testament, we note that our Lord gave a certain primacy to the teaching authority of his church. For instance, in Matthew 28:20, we see our Lord commissioning the Apostle to go and teach in his name, making disciples of all nations. That was how the word Catholic faith came about. When our Lord Jesus Christ said all nations, he meant evangelizing the world. Or if you want to put it in another way, He meant evangelizing the universe. But as you know, at the time Christ established his church, the Jews refused to accept His message. It was the gentles that accepted it. And the gentles were mostly the Greeks and the Romans. That period also Israel was under the Roman Empire and the Romans were also trying to make their language, Latin, a universal language. And so it was only natural that the church was named in Latin especially when Peter, the first Pope decided to evangelize Rome. The Latin word for universe is called 'Catholicus' which was also gotten from the Greek word 'katholikos' meaning universal. But the stupid question people ask these days is: when Jesus established the church did he name it Catholic? They are forgetting that before the Bible was written in English, it had been translated into three languages before English. The

New Testament originally was written in Aramaic language, the language of Palestine at the time of Christ. Thereafter, it was translated into Greek and from Greek into Latin. It was in Latin for almost 16 centuries before the reformation. It was during the formation it was translated into English. So the word 'Catholicus' or Catholic means universal and when you say Catholic Church, you are also saying a universal church. Now I believe you know how the word Catholic came about."

Edison was relieved. All along he had been finding it difficult to explain how the Catholic Church, being the first church is not in the Bible. Now he understood that universe is just the English word for the Latin word catholicus.

"Yes Father." he said. "These days you hear of abc church international as if it is some kind of business. The other day I was passing by a street when I saw this church. Guess the name of the church *Jehovah Sharp Sharp Ministry International*. What a hell of a name for a church."

The Father sighed. Edison couldn't help it but felt the pain of the father. "Ok, back to our discussion, remember the emphasis of our Lord Jesus Christ was preaching and not on printing and distributing it. Thus it follows that the leadership and teaching authority of the church are indispensable elements in the means whereby the Gospel message is to reach the ends of the earth. So tell me, since the church produced the scriptures, is it not quite biblical, logical and reasonable to say that the church alone has the authority to interpret properly and apply them?"

Edison had always known there was something unique about the Catholic faith, everlasting truth about her. That she cannot err in what she teaches. He even remembered somewhere in the scripture where Christ, after he has founded His church, said "I will be with you till the end of time and the gates of hell shall not prevail against you."

"I agree with you father." Edison said. "This is funny", the father continued :"but the scriptures itself in Timothy 3:15 called the church- that is the living community of believers founded upon St. Peter and the Apostles and headed by their successors, the pillar and ground of truth. Of course, this passage is not meant in anyway to diminish the importance of the Bible but it is intending to show that Jesus Christ did establish an authoritative teaching church which was commissioned to teach all nations. By virtue of being the pillar and ground of truth it was built in such a way that the church will never in any time preach or teach anything false either in morals or doctrine. Elsewhere in the scriptures we read that Christ gave to the visible head of His church St. Peter, and later the entire apostles the keys to the kingdom of heaven. Christ said: *And I will give to thee the keys of the kingdom of heaven so that whatever thou shalt bind upon earth, it shall be bound in heaven: and whatever thou shalt loose on earth, it shall be loosed also in heaven.* Mind you, this term of binding and loosing is a Jewish terminology which means the ultimate power to pronounce Judgment on matters of faith and morals. Now tell me, is it not plainly evident from the binding and loosing terminology that our Lord wanted his church to be the final authority in matters of faith and morals?"

"Absolutely true, Father." Edison said.

The father continued: "Yet certain people are trying to undermine the teaching authority of the church. What people cannot understand is the tradition the Catholic Church is practicing; which is not in the Bible".

"To tell you the truth, I'm confused at times, Father." Edison said.

"What you must understand is that sacred tradition serve as the church's living memory. It complements our understanding of the Bible. It is a deposit of faith which reminds us and those who will come tomorrow, what the faithful in the past have always believed and how to properly understand and interpret the meaning of biblical passages. In a certain way, it is a sacred tradition which says to the reader of the Bible; *you have been reading a very important book which contains God's revelation to man; now let me explain to you how it has always been understood and practiced by believers from the very beginning.*" Father Mike checked his wristwatch "My Heaven!" he exclaimed. "It is almost 6p.m, I should be preparing for mass. Meanwhile, if you don't buy me that seven bottles of beer tomorrow, I won't give you communion on Sunday. There are so many things I would like to discuss with you as regarding the teachings of the church; let's find time so that I can enlighten you properly about the teachings of the church in respect to the Bible."

Edison was more than happy at least he would be saving his money for the seven bottle of beer. He thought again. But would the father actualy drink seven bottles of beer. "Edison" the father called the second time

"Yes Father, I'm sorry."

"What are you thinking?"

"I really appreciate the time you have given me, I was just thinking of what I've learnt today. Somehow my mind is renewed, I think I should let you go Father."

"Go in the peace of the Lord" the father said. "And to-morrow when you are well prepared, come for your confession." Edison couldn't help but think again that the father wants to drink his beer by all means.

When Edison got home he was surprised and relieved. A friend was waiting for him. Where have you been brother?" the friend asked. Edison couldn't bring himself to say he went for confession but instead he said: I learnt something today. Do you know about the Freemasons?"

"Are you kidding me, who doesn't?"

"I hear they are the ones behind the success of Jay-Z, Kean West and Lady Gaga.

"You really don't know shit about them, right?"

"You can say that again."

"Well, when Michael Jackson decided to leave the organization, they had him killed and to prove they are the ones behind Jackson's success, they picked Lady Gaga. I sing ten times better than that bitch, yet her last album sold over a 100 million copies which was three times higher than the highest Jackson ever sold.

"Wait, don't tell me they had Jackson killed."

"Jackson is small potatoes; they have done worse."

"Damn" Edison cursed.

"You can say that again." the friend replied.

Chapter 7

LOVE, somebody once said, sank when the Titanic ship sank. But come to think of it, what the heck or better still, what the devil is love? Love has so betrayed the world that one is seen as a schmuck if he marries because of love. There are even some Sicilians who will slice your throat in the twinkle of an eye if you tell them love is good. For some people, any mention of love makes them wary. Like they are in some kind of danger. In the military, where men are men, there is no room for love or compassion. Ranking officers blow smoke to make their subjects loyal.

And this is true for love; for what good is love without respect or obedience.

Even Christ said: *If you love me, keep my commandments.* That statement alone summarizes what is called *constructive love.* But where people got the idea of *you –must- be-like -Romeo and Juliet-* before the love can be true beats the imagination. A man's primary duty is to earn a living. When that is established, the next thing for him is to make sure there is a family to enjoy the proceeds of his hard work with. For what greater love can there be than to sacrifice oneself and enjoy the proceeds of one's sacrifice with one's family. Remaining faithful to his wife, making sure she and the children are well fed, clothed and sheltered. But for a full blooded youth, he should be able to know those little things, a woman needs and provide them. It is those little things that mean more to them. Any form of sexual immorality between them complicates the issue and most times destroys the relationship. This kind of love becomes destructive. It should not be trusted. Even Machiavelli had this to say about love: *I say that a prince must want to have a reputation for compassion rather than for cruelty: nonetheless, he must be careful that he does not make bad use of compassion: in other words, for the question whether it is better to be loved than feared or vise vaser the answer is that according to Machiavelli, one would like to be both the one and the other, but because it is difficult to combine them, it is far better to be feared than loved if you cannot be both.* Although this answer was for the rulers of kingdom, nonetheless, it can also be applied by those who are heads of family, heads of large conglomerates, or in any circle where one has subjects.

Desmond, the big eye of the Buccaneers Confraternity knew this to a certain degree. He knew as a man, that there is no room for love at least not in the worldly terms. He knew as a man especially if one is a fratman that one can't afford to be soft or be sentimental. That sentiment was for suckers. But he couldn't help himself with the way he was feeling for his new found love, Ivie Amadason. It was supposed to be a game to get at Jackson but in the process he fell in love. Or perhaps he thought so. And that was always the problem for him; where to draw the line between love and lust. For there is a thin line between love and lust. As for Ivie, no doubt she had got class; not only that, she was good in bed. But each time he thought about her and the feeling he had for her, he always remembered that line Mario Puzo used in *The Last Don* about Croccifixio. The line reads: *It was the beginging of the end, crossifixio De Lena fell in love at first sight.* What was he to do? Obviously she's in love. But who can be sure of that?

The second semester had just resumed and so almost everbody was back to campus. He decided to call her and see if she had left Lagos where she resided.

"Hi Ivy." He called her pet name.

"Hi baby." she responded.

"What are you still doing in Lagos, don't you know I have missed you so?"

"What the fuck are you yakking about? I'm in campus and I have missed you too, you know."

"Oh! I didn't know, why don't you come over here, sit on my lap then we'll talk about the first thing that pops up?"

She giggled. "I already know the first thing that will pop up."

"What do you mean, are you now a clairvoyant?"

"You bet. With my lovely ass on your laps what do you think will pop up first?"

"You are so smart, that's why I love you."

"I've got a present for you. I'm gonna suck the blood out of you like you're never been sucked before."

"Wow! I can't wait baby. It's been a long time I was really sucked. Do me a favour, stop whatever you are doing and board a bike down here. Ok?"

"Yeah, copy that. See you in less than ten minutes." At that they ended the call.

In Ambrose Alli University, Ekpoma, after the renunciation of fraternity members, the ground became peaceful. In order for this peace to remain forverer, a crusade was formed by ex-cult members to fight cultism. The school authority backed them up. Guns where given to the excos for protection. This was to help cult activities to be wiped out or if possible, to be submerged. The name of this crusade or organization was 'ACCON' an acronym for Anti-Cult Crusade Organization of Nigeria. In time they became so powerful. This was due to their secrecy and the backing of the school authority. Only excos were known. Others for fear that cult members shouldn't attack them subbed their identity. Even dreaded cult members were scared. The Acconites were elated, they began to do as they please. When a suspected cult member was reported to them, they in turn report the person to the school authority. When a proper investigation is carried out and the person is found quilty, the school rusticates him. This went on for a while, thus forcing fratertnity members to go underground. Cult activities became secret once more again.

Beverly Hills Hotel was one of the best night clubs in Ekpoma. As at 2004 every Friday night was their party night: ladies go in for free but guys for a token fee are allowed to enter. It was a way of reducing their stress after a hectic week of school stress. Most people were glad for the opportunity. There they got free asses and boobs while dancing and if some are lucky, these ladies will use them. Yes, during that time it was usually the ladies that do the fucking.

Then, any attempt to woo a lady may result to rustication if care was not taken. These ladies seeing that cult wings have been broken were now bold. If a guy tries to woo them and they don't like the guy, they report him to the Acconites who in turn report the person to the school authority. A disciplinary committee was set up to judge the person's case and if found guilty, the person would be rusticated. A minimum of three examples had been shown by the school authority forcing others to be wise. Now nobody wanted trouble, all they want was to graduate without trouble.

So on this particular Friday night at Beverly Hills, this guy was dancing with a lady as usual. Holding those places that needed to be held. But all of a sudden, the lady turned around and slapped him. The guy was an Axeman. He couldn't believe it. His own rugged brothers were around watching. Knowing full well that forgiveness was a sin, he knew he cannot allow the lady to go scot-free but what was he to do? If he doesn't do anything then, his rugged brothers would treat his fuck-up after the party. He quickly made up his mind. It was so quick she didn't see it coming. The next thing she would see was darkness all around her with tiny little stars dancing in the darkness. The slap was so real she couldn't belive it. Much to her shock, another landed on the second side of her face which sent her sprawling on the floor and what more, more came after that which resulted to a broken tooth. Although she was on the floor it didn't stop the blows and slaps that was raining on her. The guy was so angry he was investing all the rage inside him on her. When others tried to interfere, his rugged brothers quickly rose up to protect him. In the end, the lady was nothing to write home about. But that wasn't the end of it; the lady reported to the Acconities, they traced the guy, got him and presented him to the school authority. The school authority didn't bother to waste time on his case. He was expelled immediately.

———— ◦«◦»◦ ————

Before the arrival of Ivie Amadason, the first shipmate of the deck came to see his big eye. Now that the deck had set for sail, certain issues must be discussed to move the deck forward.

"Alora me shipmate." the big eye said. "Welcome back to deck. How was the two weeks break for you?"

"Thanks to G.P it was smooth sailing for me. How about you?"

"Smooth sailing for me except I didn't get the chance to invite all the deckhands for my father's 50th birthday celebration."

"Yeah, that lubbish grove was rugged. We all drank and ate to our satisfaction."

"Talking about grove, we need to start preparing for it. How much do you think we should cut?" the big eye asked.

"Depends on the kind of food and drinks we are to serve and the number of Lords present on deck."

"We are about 80 Lords present and I intend to make this groove a tested one. You know we gotta keep up with the tradition of doing the most rugged groove every session."

"I can feel you brother." His shipmate said.

"I would like us to buy a cow."

"To get a good size cow, we should be talking about 80-90 grand. And for drinks, that should another 40-50 grand."

"What of transportation for the ladies?" the big eye asked.

"Five grand will take care of that."

"What else?"

"You haven't talked about souvenir."

"Yeah what do think we should use?"

"Last time we used buckets; so this time we should use something different."

At that moment they heard a knock at the entrance gate. The big eye got up to see who was there. It was no other person than Ivie herself. Seeing her made him happy like a pig in shit.

"Hi baby, thought it was gonna take you forever to come."

"Are you kidding me? I was quicker than a shit off a shovel." She said.

"Well, come on in. By the way, how much milk have you been drinking?"Desmond asked.

"What?"

"I know milk does the body good. But yours is too good to be true. Something tells me you've been drinking more milk than necessary."

"Are you complaining?" she asked,

"That's the point, I can eat you alive."

She went inside while Desmond was locking the gate.

"Hey! She said to the person inside.

"Dessy, you didn't tell me you had a friend in here. I was about stripping off my clothes.

"Hey Honey," Desmond was inside now.

"Behave, you don't want my friend to see those great boobs of yours. Do you? Trust me, he is as scared of holding those boobs as much as he is scared of holding his dick while pissing."

"Right now, what the boob needs is someone to hold and caress them. If you ain't gonna do it then I believe your friend can, right?" she asked Desmond's friend.

"You bet your ass I can baby."

"Charles." Desmond called his first shipmate.

"Please meet my girlfriend, Ivie."

"Ivie, meet my friend Charles."

"Nice to meet you." Both said at the same time.

"Honey I like your friend already, he is bold."

"Hey baby, all my friends are bold but what is this thing about like?"

"Dessy, like is just like ok? It is not going to grow beyond that stage."

"Well you make sure it does not grow beyond."

With the way the conversation was going Charles was nervous as a dog in a room full of rocking chairs. Nervous in the sense that if the girl gives him the green light, he might not be able to resist approaching her. He told his big eye: "I've got to go to the school café to register my school fees pin before the card gets lost."

"Ok then. I'll come over later. Meanwhile float my ideas to the rest DMs and see their response. Let's try and see tomorrow to discuss the way forward."

"Ok." Charles replied

"S.O me bro" the Big eye said .Charles echoed his response.

Ivie was happy. She has achieved her aim.

"Hey baby, why are you smiling? You look like you have won a million naira." Desmond said.

"You wouldn't know."

"Well, whatever. Why not come over here on my lap and we discuss life."

She got up to meet him. But instead of sitting on his lap, she started unzipping his fly.

———— ◦《◦》◦ ————

If human nature doesn't surprise you every once in a while then you have not known it. The problem with most humans is by the time you make them feel they are your equal, they immediately begin to think they are your superiors. Worse still is when a lady begins to treat you like shit. Like a piece of crap. But then there are many men who because of pussy, become children. They loose their sense of reasoning and as a result they become foolish. They let the whim of pussy control their lives. But this particular frat guy, a Maphite in question was more rugged than most of his peers. Why he was more a man was because he doesn't allow what Iies between a woman's legs to control his life; unlike some of his peers who later came to their own ruin because of pussy.

His girlfriend named Rita, for some time now had been loyal, she washes his clothes cooks for him each time she comes to his house and clean his room. For all these she was protected by Rakim the Maphite. But because women are who they are, she couldn't withstand the pressure of guys frolicking around her. On a number of occasions when she's busy chatting with her male friends all he had to do was pass by and she would break up her discussion and follow him. But after some time she didn't see any reason why she should break up her discussion with these male friends of hers, to follow her boyfriend Rakim.

Rakim noticed all these but didn't say anything. He was that kind of a guy. Next he observed she wasn't coming to his apartment to help him with his domestic work. She only went once in while and even at that, she refuses his sex advances. Although any form of care was contrary to Rakim's nature, nonetheless he manages to make others listen to his feelings. That was what got Rita. She couldn't figure out how she fell in love with Rakim. Others on the contrary shew a direct tender care which sweeps her off her feet but that was what Rakim was not good at.

"Hey Rakim, what's the problem?' his friend Bobby was asking. "You've been like this since I came. Care to share?"

"Is it so obvious? I feel so terrible right now. I'm embarrassed to say this."

"What?" Bobby asked.

"It's my girl. She's putting on an attitude I can't seem to understand. She knows she's the only one I've got."

"Ok if you want me to talk to her, I'ma do that for you. She is a good kid. Maybe she is going through stress."

But the reaction of Rakim surprised Bobby. He turned sharply and said.

"Don't do it. I'ma do it myself. If you do it, it will look like I can't handle my shit. You feel me?"

"Hey Dawg, just so you know I'm here for you whatever

the trouble; you dig?"

"Yeah man. That's why you are my real real." And they shook hands together. Then Bobby left.

Although Bobby wasn't a fratman, he was rugged in his own fashion. He was not to know Rakim is a fratman. Rakim at first never wanted his friendship but because Bobby kept coming to him, he had no choice but to be his friend. Soon they became close pals. Although he distrusted his high spiritedness but because it didn't get in the way of their friendship, they became even closer.

Oddly enough, Rakim was a rock fan. Maybe because of his sober nature. One of his best rock artistes was Linkin Park. If there's anything Rakim loves about Linkin Park, it is the way Linkin Park screams. Like it has been in him for too long and he couldn't keep it any longer.

This particular track "NUMB" was one of his best. He loves the lyrics of the song in a way the message of the song is almost similar to his life. His father who was a medical doctor wanted him to be a medical doctor as well but he loves to draw. He is good at it and he knows that. When he told his father he wanted to be an artist, his father's words were; "Not in my house. *Have you gone nuts? What the heck is wrong with you? Look at the average Nigerian, do you think he cares about art work? Look Sonny be sensible, I want the best for you ok? I don't want you to starve. How many houses have you been to that display art work? Don't disappoint me Sonny. If at least you don't want to be a medical doctor, be in the medical field. There are lots of disciplines in the medical field you can choose from. There is pharmacy, dentistry, medical lab science, bio chemistry, and lots more. Look, I've seen many artists beg for food but how many doctors have you seen begging for food?*" But Rakim stood on his decision. When the father saw that the situation was hopeless he said: "The only way I can sponsor your education is if you read Architecture." Rakim agreed and it was settled.

He was thinking about his life when he heard a knock at door.

When he opened the door he was surprised to find Rita.

"Hello Rita." he said, "I didn't expect to see you. Is something biting you?" Rita wondered for the hundreth time again what made her fall in love with Rakim. Although she knows she is beautiful but Rakim seemed to be the only one not to notice it. Like he didn't care. She knew of a millions guys that would hug her and pet her but not Rakim. When she was seated inside she asked; "Rakim do you love me?"

The question threw Rakim aback:

"What kindda question is that?"

"I need to know." she said.

"Don't fuck with me baby."

"You don't care for me I can see it."

"Damn, we've been going out now for since like God knows when and I've never cheated on you since we began this relationship. How come you say you don't know it? Even Steven Wonder can see it.

"Give me a straight answer and stop beating about the bush. Moreover I need you to turn down the volume of your music. Why do you even play this kind of music anyway? It's for the white folks. What has happened to our local jams that we do here?"

"The volume stays that way and who are you to tell me what to like or hate?"

"That's your funeral. Are you going to give me my answer you weak ass boy? I'm getting fed up here. I shouldn't have come." It was so fast she didn't know how it happened. But the next thing she heard was a slap on her face that got one of her tooth shaking.

"Rakim did you just slap me?"

"You'll earn another if you talk out of turn again"

"Is this how you prove to me you love me? Go out there and see how real men are taking care of their girlfriends. You are only a boy and not a man so you wouldn't know what love is. It was a mistake I fell in love with you. All those other guys are far better than you."

Another two slaps was recorded on her face that got her crying.

"If you think I'm not good enough for you then get the fuck outta her. You've been whoring yourself around, you bitch. You think they love you. They will use you and dump you. But me, I've been faithful to you since we started this thing, only you are too dumb to know it. Get outta her I don't want to see you again."

She slowly got up, picked up her bag and left.

But of course Rakim was still in love with her. He just couldn't understand how everything got this way. He was at sea of what to do to bring her back. He checked his cigarette case but the last one has been smoked by him before Rita came. He got up to go to his friend's place. By the time he got to Bobby's place he was already calmed down. 'Africa queen' by 2face Idibia was playing out loud from bobby's apartment.

Bobby's parents were top politicians in the country. So it was easy for Bobby to have access to easy money. While most students stuck to a room off campus, a few managed to get themselves a self contained apartment but Bobby was living in a two bedroom flat that was well furnished. At one time when he brought a car to school, he almost got himself killed. Other frat men began to think he was a Maphite because he was rolling with Rakim who was a signboard in school. The Maphites had hit one of the Vikings men but he didn't die. The Vikings, in retaliating cornered Bobby. Bobby pleaded with his life that he was not a Maphite. Nevertheless, he sustained some bruises from an angry mob rough handling him. His luck was that the hit man holding the pump action wasn't the trigger happy type. After the incident, he knew better than to roll with Rakim 24/7. He asked Rakim if he is a Maphite but Rakim denied it flat. When he took the car home at the end of that semester, he never brought it again.

Rakim was inside the house now. He didn't like it that Bobby was not security conscious. Anything can happen in Ekpoma. People can get killed just because some trigger happy frat men want to test their new weapons. It is not safe to open one's doors. It is not as if he was throwing a party. *I am going to talk some sense into him Rakim told himself.* Opening the door of his bedroom, he was saying "Bobby what the fuck is wrong….." Than he paused. What he saw staggered him a little. On the bed was Bobby and Rita half naked.

"Fuck" Rakim said "Bobby I thought you were my friend. Now I see you've been stabbing me in the back."

"Shit." Bobby said. Look dawg, I can explain."

"Fuck off, I ain't your dawg." and Rakim slammed the door shut and left.

"Damn!" Bobby cursed. "What am I gonna do?" he has

known Rakim long enough to know that Rakim was the merciless type. If he doesn't act now he's gonna stew in his own juice. He quickly got up, wore his clothes asked Rita to leave and pursued Rakim. When finally, he got to Rakim's house, he knelt down to beg Rakim to forgive him.

"What you saw was not really what was happening." He was telling Rakim.

"We were just, I mean I was"

"I don't want to hear of it just go." Rakim said.

"Whatever amends I'ma do for your forgiveness I'ma do. You just let me know."

Rakim was thinking, 'does he think it is as easy as that? But when he replied him he said: "Look I forgive you but I don't want to see you again."

"Thank you dawg."

"Hey! Don't you get it, I ain't your dawg, fuck off. You are irritating me."

"Thanks da… thanks, I'ma make it up to you." Then he left. He knew for a fact that Rakim is a Maphite, and a strong Maphite at that. In fact his denying it emphasized it more strongly that he was a Maphite. Two week later Bobby was bloodied by unknown gun men. The order was, "don't kill him but that was the mistake. Whenever anyone wants to deal with an enemy, he has to deal with him in such a way that will render the person useless to fight back. The best way most times is by whacking. That way you can be sure there won't be any revenge that is if the person is a bloody civilian but if the person is a frat guy, one thinks twice before doing anything because once the person's family or fraternity discovers who did it then there ain't no telling the shit that will happen. That's why it is better to be a fratman or a family man or whatever you might want to call it than to be a bloody civilian, lubber, Jew or bastardo as the Vikings call those not in any family in school.

When finally he came out of the coma, he was surprised to find people surrounding his bed. Bandage covered most part of his body. The first thing he said was a question.

"Where am I, and what are you people doing here?"

It was the ACCON number 2 man that replied him. He said.

"You are lucky. If one of us didn't see you as at the time he saw you, who knows, maybe you would have been dead. You were discovered in front of your house around 20:00 hrs on the ground with wounds and cuts all over your body. You seem to have lots of blood. Blood was all over the place. We didn't think you would make it. Now can you remember who did this to you?"

It took a long time before Bobby answered; when he answered it was single word. "Rakim."

The ACCON number 2 asked

You mean Rakim the Maphite? The guy you use to roll with?"

"Yes." was all Bobby could say.

When Rakim was abducted by the ACCONITIES, he was given the same treatment that was given to Bobby, but of course, a military man cannot be compared to a civilian. Before becoming a Maphite, he had undergone a similar drill to prepare him for the times ahead. It would have been a fuck up on his part if he had fainted. But before he was taken to the school authority, he had been cleaned up. When the school authority reviewed his case, they found him guilty and rusticated him for two years.

———»«(»)«———

All the deck masters of the Buccaneers Confraternity, assembled in the big eye's house.

The Big eye ordered a crate of Star beer which they took to the back of his house. On a round table, the discussion started.

"Alora me big eye" the steerer of the deck was calling his big eye. "Your 1st shipmate told us about the plan for a rugged S.T. We've analyzed it and concluded that N200,000.00 will take care of it."

"Will that take care of food, drinks souvenir and transport?" the big eye asked

"Yeah, all the angles have been figured out. Out of the 200 grand, 45% will be for meat, drinks will take 25%, transport 2.5% and souvenirs 27.5%."

"What did you agree to use for souvenir?" the big eye asked.

"A mini towel with our emblem on it. We figured 200 quantities should be ok but if you are not satisfied with the quantity let us know."

"No it's ok." the big eye said. "That way everybody gets. The ladies and the Lords. Alora ff how much is in the account?"

"Alora me big eye, we only have 50 grand in the account."

The Big eye sighed.

"Alora steerer, there are about 80 sailing Lords on deck How much will each cut to amount to 260 grand?"

"Two thousand, five hundred naira." The Big eye nodded his head. He seemed to be far in thought. All the deckmasters were waiting for him. When he came back from his soul travel he turned to the KMS. "Alora KMS, of course you are aware that this semester, we'll be conducting an induction ceremony for our lubbers. Start gathering them. Our first JJ will be two weeks from now" "How much are we charging our lubbers?" the KMS asked.

"Twenty grand would be a cheap price for lubbers to become Lords."

The steerer quickly cut in. Alora big eye, not everybody is born with a sliver spoon some of us are born with mud spoons. The Big eye laughed out loud. "Mud spoon eh? Is there anything like mud spoon?" The big eye was asking. "So how much do you think we should reduce it to?"

"In my book, I'll say 10 grand."

"Nah nah, that's too cheap, these lubbers want to be Lords and becoming a Lord comes with a price. You must understand that. Ok? Let's not fight ourselves over lubbers. They ain't worth it. Fifteen grand would be cheap. These lubbers will becomes Lords in a silver platter."

The house echoed their response. "My big eye has capped." The KMS said and that ended it. Lubbers will pay fifteen grand.

"Alora DMs," the big eye continued. "It is not my pleasure to see Lords complain of Fs. After they must have bought their handout, textbooks, feed and transport themselves to and fro school, we would be practicing BKB (brother kill

Brother) asking them to cut two thousand, five hundred naira each. Although I know very well they can afford three times the amount if necessary but it is not wise to do something others can do for you and so by the power bestowed on me by G.P, I say all Lord should cut one thousand five hundred naira as the ST dues."

'Gboyaga, dancekelebe, chiakwu, crook ku roo' the house was jubilating. "Our big eye is rugged." When the jubilating calmed down, the big eye continued;

"Like I said, it is not rugged to do things others can do for you. The balance of the money will be gotten from our lubber's pocket. After all, that's why they are lubbers."

The house echoed their response.

"Alora DMs, there is still another issue I would like us to discuss. Most of us will be *salted* very soon. I'll like us to leave a mark behind. I've been thinking of buying waste bins, place it at strategic positions, and one in each department. On it will be written courtesy BAN (Buccaneers across Nigeria). How does the idea sound?"

"The idea is rugged" the hauler answered him, but we just jubilated that you've made sailing easy for us by slashing our ST dues down to one thousand, five hundred naira, only for you to bring this up again. Getting a good waste bin will cost us money and that will mean more contribution, except you've got other ways to raise the money. The big eye was nodding his head and smiling curiously. Like he was thinking *why is it that most people don't like to contribute to the general good of the society,* but he said; "We have some money in the account right, FF?

"Yeah." the ff replied.

That reminds me" the big eye continued; "has all the Lords cut their deck dues?"

"No" the ff replied.

"What! What is wrong with Lords these days, they squander two to three thousand naira drinking beer when they take their girlfriends to eateries, they spend nothing less than 3,000 naira and yet they can't cut their dues of 1,000 naira .Do you have the list of those who haven't cut their dues?"

"Yeah"

"Ok, take two or three DMS with you after this MIT and dive those lords. Embarrass them if necessary. Since they don't want to respect themselves, they should be embarrassed so that all their girlfriends should see them that they are owing. You feel me?"

"Yeah, Alora me big eye." the FF replied.

"Well, now that this is settled, I'll like to know if anybody has any observation to make." The KMS indicated.

"Alora big eye, Alora deck masters, all other protocols observed. I, Alora KMS of the deck, it is my duty to ensure that all debts are squared. We all know that the Axe men and the Bird Boys have priced us. We can't allow them to go scot free without them paying the price. I say all hands must be on deck to ensure a smooth and rugged sailing this semester." The house echoed their response. The KMS continued: "As for plans to hit these high lubbers I'm yet to hear from my big eye."

There was murmuring in the house. All were waiting for the big eye to say something. The big eye, in turn was waiting for the murmuring to die down. When the murmuring finally died down, he said: "Alora deck masters, I feel your pain, if only you can see through me, you would know that the façade I'm putting on is a scam. I understand your agitation. In BAN, there is what is called BLOOD FOR BLOOD. May GP never forgive me if I fail to carry out my duties? But again think of those times we've had RS (rough sea) in the past. Have you forgotten what happened at Barbados between Lords and the Bird Boys? Have you forgotten that it was two years later that Lords struck back? Can you still remember the saga of Hawaii between Lords and the KKK? Where Lords struck back a year later, what of Gaza's Trip at least that should be fresh in your memory where Lords had to hit the Maphites six months later or is it in Reveria where Lords whacked the Axe men three top excos including their number I a year later after they hit a Lord. Of course you can still remember the saga of Cayman deck where the arm of a Bird boy was cut off because he slapped a Lord. If I start citing examples we'll not leave here. Look, I'm not trying to glory in these things but when people push you to the wall, you have no choice but to fight. Your life may depend on it. Look, I want you all to calm down, I promise you before the semester runs out, we'll hit".

The house echoed their response.

The Big eye sighed again.

"Now that this is settled, anything else?"

The house seemed to be at rest. Since nobody had anymore observation, the big eye toasted the DMs although it was with a beer. Only the big eye had a glass of beer, the rest prefered to guzzle from the bottle. Odd as it may seem, some Lords do not drink or smoke or even womanize which is common among youths. So among the Deck masters, two out of them did not touch their beer.

The big eye raised his glass of beer and said: "Here is to a successful semester, may we sail and never get marooned, may we sail to discover our treasure, may the dangling swords of G.P be our source of ruggedity, May through the practice of BDB deliver us from our enemies and may G.P guide and protect us as we sail to greater heights." For each of the prayers the house echoed their traditional response. The big eye welcomed them on board once more again and bade them to sail on.

"Sail on alora me rugged big eye." They returned.

<hr />

The ACCON, by late 2003 had become so strong that one cannot tell the difference between them and frat men. Power is a dangerous thing! Although good in itself but if in the wrong hands, it can be as fatal as a bullet through the heart. ACCON had become so powerful they began to act like the frat men they were before. For the most stupid of reasons, they dive anybody, beat the person mercilessly and as if that is not enough, they burn the person's belongings. It happened once too often.

Obaze, popularly called 'Obaze the scam' was a very funny and jovial guy. He was a Bird boy. At one time he impregnated a girl, Jumoke; when the girl discovered that she was pregnant she came to him, "Obaze, I have got something to tell you."

"Come on Jumoke. You nor see say I dey read, we get test tomorrow why you wan disturb me now?

"I beg the thing dey important."

"*Which kind thing they important pass test again now?*" Obase asked.

"*I go hospital and doctor say I don get belle and na you fuck me last before the belle come.*"

"*You say wetin?*" Obaze asked.

"*Na you fuck me last before the belle come.*" she repeated again.

"*You still dey talk am, nor be you fuck me? Now you con dey talk say na me fuck you. Shey that day I tell you say I nor wan fuck but you say we must fuck. Now see wetin you con dey tell me. I know say forces dey against me. The other day, my papa for the 1st time give me garri come school. When I drink the garri, the garri be wan kill me. Na my friends kon persuade me to go throway the gari. I no blame the man; he marry three wives and him children be like 17 so he wan try reduce them so that he go fit take care of the ones wey go remain. See, Jumoke, my papa don try to kill me but he no fit. Now you wan try your own. Eh? Why you dey do me like this? You wan spoil my life abi? Abi you nor see say na manage I dey manage myself for this school wey I dey go. Na with luck I dey eat two square meal a day. Most times na one. Now how you wan make I take feed pikin when I never fit feed myself?*"

Jumoke became helpless, she pitied him. Frankly, Obaze was one of the best in his department. Why should she spoil a good man's life? She began to feel guilty although it wasn't her fault. Finally she said; "*Ok, I go go for abortion. I go look for half of the money and make you try look for the other half too so that we go fit do this abortion otherwise make you ready buy Cerelac.*" Obaze agreed. When he told his friends the story later, they laughed and laughed.

The Vikings Confraternity, a confraternity which was originated by a former member of the Buccaneers Confraternity started their operations from the University of Portharcourt, River state. They were rugged to the core. In the Vikings ship, anything goes just to survive. One of the rudiments to becoming a Viking is that one must be a thief of some sort. During initiations, one is asked to steal something and bring it to the ship before he can proceed to the final test. During initiations something of a barbaric nature is instilled into them so that once they become kings, they become a throwback of their old ancestors. Those barbaric Kings who controlled empires way back. When the Roman Empire was destroyed, the people from Scandinavia became the pirates in power. These were the Vikings which mean "pirate men". Oddly enough, they were talented, they were called poets, story tellers, ruthless conquerors, explorers, plunderers and barbarians. Most of them were from Denmark, Norway and Sweden. They sailed the seas between the eight to eleventh centuries and most countries were afraid of them. Some people called them the Norsemen or Northman. Their ship, long in length moved through the water either by sail and wind or by slaves who rowed the boat quickly through the water, they were known for making slaves out of the crews of ships captured from Christian countries like England and France.

So, it was only natural that the spirit of the Vikings that reincarnated in Nigeria should model itself after the ancestors of old. In the University of Portharcourt, they became so terrifying that Bastardoes had no choice but to join them. Like in the saying, "If you can't beat them, join them." Throughout the town of Portharcourt, they spread terror. Rumour had it that at least five former state governors of River State were Vikings. Although the Axemen were their greatest rival, nonetheless the Axemen suffered a great deal of loss fighting the Vikings. The Klansmen Konfraternity, in the other to expand their influence created "street and creek" wing DEEBAM to combat Vikings in the streets. When it seemed they were gaining some territories of the Vikings, the Viking created a street and creek wing of their own called DEWELL. When Dewell was unable to beat Deebam, another offshoot was created by the Vikings called Icelanders which would eventually be led by the militia leader Ateke Tom. Of course Ateke Tom and his exploits is not news. The whole world knows about him. It was through him the Vikings got control of the streets again. The Vikings had a great role to play in the Niger Delta militant sruggle. They controlled the governmewnt. They were that powerful. In the streets around the campus area, the Vikings disarms anybody, Bastardoes and frat men alike. Be you an Axemen, a Birdboy, a Buccaneer or whatever. The rule is: don't pass their territory, or else you pay some tax for passing. Tax like cell phones, one's shoes, one's belt and even one's trousers and shirts if it is good enough. Although this act had caused wars between them and other confraternities, nevertheless, they continued with their escapade.

Some how, if truth be told, they were the real pirates; because the pirates of old and even now are sea robbers. They steal from any ship. The Buccaneers of old only attacked Spanish ships. In contrast with their elder brothers in Nigeria that is, the pyrates and Buccaneers, the Vikings had no use for morality: they steal from anybody be it their father, mother, brother or whoever. And if necessary, they kill. Their ruggedity was limited to the eastern part of Nigeria. In the south, they are more careful because if truth be told nobody is a superman that cannot be killed. They piped low and do their thing. In Ambrose Alli University, Ekpoma when ACCON was so powerful, acting as they pleased, they published a list of members of different confraternities to face disciplinary committee either for rustication or expulsion. Of course the Axemen and Bird Boys had the highest number followed by the Maphite before the Buccaneers. These were the major confraternities in the South South region of Nigeria. The Vikings were not included but they were warned that they are being watched. It was ruggedity on their part. For if truth be told, it is not easy to control a large number of youths with blood running in their veins. If a person can do that, then that person is fit to be called a genius. It is for this reason the Pyrates and Buccaneers are the most rugged. According to a paper in Nigeria, these two confraternities are the Godfather confraternities while the rest were termed cultists and terrorists.

During renunciation, a certain Viking named Ebojie renounced. He didn't really know why he renounced. After the whole renunciation exercise had died down, he began to see the consequences of his renunciaton. First his rugged brothers snubbed him but that could be understood. Worse was: he no longer had access to information regarding war. As sailors, (the Vikings addressed themselves as sailors just as the Buccaneers and Pyrates address themselves as SeaLords and Sea Dogs) One was expected to read the weather and tell if a storm was approaching. This of course was the main duty of the captain of a ship. Then he passeed the information to members of the crew or deckhands to be ready. If the storm was of such magnitude that would sink the ship, everybody would be advised to abandon ship (ABS). In contrast, confraternity men or sailors were expected to read the weather and tell if a storm was approaching. The magnitude of the storm determineed if the sailors were to weather the storm or ABS. In other words, they are to observe from a point to see if trouble was looming. If the trouble was such that they cannot handle, then the deck master would do what they have to do to survive. For the deckhands, they are advised to ABS if they cannot withstand the storm. This was the major problem he was facing. He was no longer given signal of looming war about to happen so that he could run to a place of safety. On various occasions, attempts were made to kill him. The only thing that saved him was luck. When he reasoned that the whole thing out, he discovered that the best thing to do would was to go back to his rugged brothers. But then that was another problem of itself again. Who knows what he may be asked to steal this time; perhaps the vice chancellor's pen. Even this was good compared to the match he was going to pass through all over again. Of course, he is a Bastardo to them and if he was going to become a Viking again, he was going to pass through the three stages again. He barely survived his initiation to become a Viking then. In that match three bastardos fainted and because of that they were not initiateded. Fact of the matter is, the Vikings initiation drill is one of the most violent among the other fraternities. There is 90 percent chance that he may even be killed during the initiation. What was he to do? He kept asking himself that he cannot start all over again. He knew that, so he started contacting some of his pals still in the game. When he saw them for a friendly chat, he would chip in one two Vikings' language hoping they would forgive him and would put in a word to indicate that he was still interested in the game. This continued for a while until the Vikings officers got wind of his intention. On a fateful day, he was with his friends (Vikings) again chatting. It wasn't up to 15 minutes when a car with four men inside pulled up in front of the house. When they stepped out, he was glad that he knew two of them. It was around 15:00hrs. When they entered the house they greeted their own brother the traditional way and clawed him as a sailor. When Ebojie brought his hand forward for a handshake, he got another thing entirely. It was a blow he received in the eye. When he tried to complain, the rest pounced on him like cats on a mouse. The next thing he knew, he was surrounded by family members as well as some strange peoples in a hospital. The first words he heard *was thank God* from his parents. Meanwhile the ACCON were itching to get Ebojie his justice. They couldn't wait anymore.

"Who did this to you?" one them asked. Ebojie was quiet for like five minutes. He couldn't remember anything. All he could remember was his visit to his friend Obaze. He simply said; "Obaze."

What happened next was not worth it.

The ACONITES, thinking it is the popularly known Obaze, Obaze the scam, the Bird boy, didn't waste anymore time. Immediately, they went to his house off campus. Unfortunately, he was at home playing chess with a pal of his. The next thing Obaze would hear was the kicking of his door in a violent way to open it. When they entered,

Obaze was saying, *what is happening, what is happening?* But the ACCONITES didn't borther to answer him. This time around, the friend who was playing chess was no where to be found. He seemed to have vanished into thin air. Nonetheless, the ACCONITES pounced on Obaze mercilessly. While this was going on, some were busy gathering his clothes, school files and any of his belongings for burning. The brutality the ACCONITES used in pouncing on him was too much that Obaze couldn't withstand it. He died instantly though the ACCONITES thought he was faking it. They burnt his things and left. Obaze was as good as somebody who never existed. Since there was no proof that the ACCONITES were responsible, the school authority couldn't do anything to apprehend the culprits. But not the fraternities. They didn't need proof. In their kind of Judicial system, proof is not necessary. When the Eiye Confraternity analyzed the whole thing, they knew who was responsible. A word was sent to the other fraternities that their brother had been killed unjustly. That they would need their help in the action they are about to take. When the other fraternities agreed, a motion was set for revenge.

As at 2003, in Ambrose Alli University only about 40 percent was developed in her total land area. Bushes surrounded the school and so it was natural that foot path be created to navigate one's way outside the school without going through the gate. Also that same year or perhaps that period from 2002-2005, admission was a racket that pays. Everybody was into it. The vice chancellor, the deputy, the academic and non academic staff, lecturers and even students were into it. For admitting a student, one can get as much as 50-100 grand depending on his or her sales talk; all sorts of people began to gain admission into the school. Riff-raffs, holigans and the likes became undergraduates. Although it backfired on the students who came in through this means, nontheless some managed to graduate. There was the case of a girl who graduated and went into the labour market. When called for an interview and was asked to write her name, she couldn't. That was a graduate who must have been writing her name since kindergarten. And so it was not unsual to have many students on campus. What the hell, even in one's department, one cannot know everybody in the class. And since the lecture rooms were small and students many, 90 percent of the students found themselves outside the lecture room, it therefore follows that some students must fail. Students' failure now became an avenue for lecturers to make extra money. Because certainly some are bound to fail. And so aside the handouts sold to students that were raking a lot of money, money was also coming in through 'blocking' a term used in the school which meant the greasing of lecturers' palms. Because certainly not everybody likes to read, some of them even had better grades than those who went to class so that they can get a seat and listen to the lecturer, and even those who took their time to read. This was because they know the price they must pay. Most of these lecturers also enjoyed free sex because some beauties were too good to resist. And so when the school seemed to be over populated, nobody seemed to care.

For protection and the smooth running of their operations,

the school gave ACCON a block in the school's hostel. The idea was that nobody would be stupid enough to harm a person in the school's premises. Because of this, the Acconites became bolder; they became like gods which nobody can touch. From their base they ran their operations without fear.

Since the last time they published a list of members of the different fraternities, members were now hiding behind their shadows. The last thing the members of the various fraternies wanted was to be expelled. And so on October 10th, 2003 during the second semester exams when everybody was in school, a busload of unmasked men alighted at the other side of the school where they had to walk a footpath into the school. It was 12:00hrs in the night. To make matters worse, there was power failure that night as usual. Getting close to the school's hotel, one of them put on a mask. Of course, most students were sleeping and the few that were awake were busy preparing for the day's exam. These men had a gallon of fuel with them. When they got to the hostel allotted to the ACCON, they poured the fuel around the building and light it up. Soon there were screams and people started running out, but unfortunately there were men waiting outside with guns. And so as the Acconites were coming out from their lodges, they were shot at one by one, like ducks in a pool of water. Fortunately or perhaps unfortunately, the main person they were after, the person in charge of field operations named Moses was no where to be found. It was not as if he was not at the scene but because it was an external operation, frat men from other schools, he was unrecognizable. One of the people they asked was the Moses himself whom they were looking for. When he discovered that they are after his life, he gave them a fake description. By the time they realized he was the one, according to the masked man, (the masked man was the only internal guy in the operation) he had gone far into the bush though he was still shot at.

In the end a dozen students died and another dozen were wounded. It was a job well done by the top fraternities that had suffered in the hands of the Acconites. Finally, ACCON was defeated. When it resurrected again it was just a facade. Nobody wanted to be associated with it anymore. They learnt their lesson the hard way. To fight evil one has to be prepared to lose one's life. Finally, ACCON came under the control of the various fraternities so that what the national commission was to the Italian Mafians, ACCON became that to the Nigerian fraternities, Ekopma chapter. The fraternities controlled it just like they controlled the Students' Union Government (SUG).

'Crime and evil,' somebody once said, "is the only thing that has survived intact the past millions of years." Anybody insane enough to fight crime will not live long enough to see the consequences. According to Mario Puzo, 'Evil started since when God was a boy', Of course government and criminals are one and the same thing. The only difference is that one is legal while the other illegal. The history of Nigeria politics is a case study. They say *someday is gonna be ok but when will that day come?* Till then you do what you have to do to survive even if it means slicing someone's throat. You think it is extreme? Analyse world government carefully and you will discover it is the same thing they do. They enrich their purses from what they slice off the masses. Nobody can get rich otherwise. Unfortunately that's the true nature of business.

Chapter 8

In those days the prosperity of poverty was overwhelming. People needed to survive. Something had to be done. Students no longer were content with what they were given by their parents, they needed to grow with the social status of the society. They needed to buy new clothes and shoes. They also needed extra money for beer. Students who were not born with silver spoons or whose fathers were not top politicians in the country had to device means of meeting up with their peers who had more than enough. Luckily, the whites had created the internet. Little by little cyber fraud became the in thing for students. With the technical know how, and the connections, one collects, if he knows his turf at least a hundred grand once in every two weeks. It was a pleasurable way to make money.

Two weeks later after the Buccaneers had their last meeting, they were assembled again. This time they were conducting the first stage of their initiation process for their lubbers. Their lubbers were 30 altogether. They were going through some screening exercise. The steerer had some forms in his hands. The forms the lubbers had filled to indicate their intention of becoming lords. The first on the list was called into a separate room with the other deck master inside. Since it was the first JJ (jaw jaw), the big eye didn't have to be there so the streerer was the person conducting it. He asked the first person as he got into the room.

"What is your name?" the person told him.

"What level are you?" the steerer asked again.

"200" the lubber replied.

He was slaped by one of the deck masters. "200 what?" the deck master asked him again.

"200 level" the lubber replied. In those days it was extremely important that lubbers intending to become Lords are not newbies in school. They must be from 200 level up ward.

"What mode of entry did you use in gaining admission into this school?"

"Through UME (University Metriculation Exam)" The lubber replied.

"What does the Acronym G.P.A stands for?"

"Grade point aggregate" the lubbers replied.

"What is your G.P.A?'

"3.21"

"Where does that place you?"

"Second class lower".

The steerer sighed. In buccaneering, it is important that one is intellectually rugged, although 3.21 as G.P is good but not good enough. Second class upper would have been better. The steerer looked at the rest DMs and they in turn returned the look. They knew why he stared at them. Second class lower doesn't favour a lubber intending to become a lord.

"Who brought you here?"

The lubber mentioned the name of the Lord that brought him there. Immediately three lords pounced on him like cats on a mouse. The deck masters where there not so much as to frighten the lubbers but to correct them in their periodical fuck ups. It is necessary a lubber doesn't mention the name of the person that mentored him or introduced him into the game. When a lubber does that he is seen as a future traitor. So the defect is quickly corrected before he becames a full member. After all there's an African adage that says, "You can tell a cock the moment it is hatched." when the DMs freed him, he was asked the same question again.

"Who brought you here?"

He paused, at sea of what to do, he began to think: why *did they pounce on me like that?* He asked himself *or is it that he didn't call the person's name with respect?* He decided to add Mr. to the person's name. When he answered, he was surprised to see five Lords pouncing on him again.

By the time they were finished with him, a tooth of his was shaking. This time around he was wise enough to know that nobody brought him there, that he came of his own doing. So when he was asked the question the third time he simple said: "Nobody."

What department are you?" the steerer asked.

"Geology."

"Who is the head of your department?

"Professor Aimufua."

"What is the name of your V.C?"

"Professor Amao."

"One final question. Supposing tomorrow you become a

lord. And you were given the signal that there is a very important MIT at a certain hour and at that same hour, you are expected to go see your sick mother at the hospital what will you do as a Buccaneer?"

The question confused him. Not so much as confused in the sense, but as to what will happen to him if he answers either way. The question was to test his IQ. He thought about it for like two minutes. When he answered, he said: "As a buccaneer, I would come for the meeting." Immediately, all the deck masters pounced on him. As they were entering him, he was shouting I'll go see my mom, I'll go see mom." but it was too late. By the time the DMS were through with him, the tooth that was shaking pulled off. Thank goodness it was in a hotel. Where he could properly clean himself. The same drill went for the rest. By the time the Deck master were through with the lubbers, they were exhausted.

"Shit! This shit is tasking." The streerer said.

"You can say that again bro." the KMS told the steerer.

"What wouldn't I do for a bottle of beer? Killing ten Axemen would be a small price to pay for a bottle beer." The hauler said.

That ain't right, you can't be comparing peoples lives with a bottle of beer. The FF replied him. "What! Are you kidding me? Those people are about as useful as a condom vending machine in Vatican". The hauler responded.

"Don't condemn people like that, some of them are useful to the society and by the way is it really true that people don't use condoms to fuck in Vatican?" The steerer was watching them like a scientist observing a new specimen. If there's anything these people like more than anything, it was pussy.

"No they don't." the hauler responded. "Go tell that to the birds." the FF replied him.

The 1st shipmate was tired of these small talks so he asked the steerer. "I thought there was some crates of beer designated for this function.

"Yeah." the steerer said" but what do you mean crates? It is just a crate"

"Jesus fucking Christ, you mean there's a crate of beer all the while and you didn't... damn!" the 1st shipmate exclaimed.

"Hey what did you just say? Jesus fucking what? Have you gone nuts? When your parents tell you not you watch too much TV, you think they don't know what they are doing? Now look at yourself. You better stop watching American movies. It ain't good for you. Damn it, you are a condemned man." The 2nd shipmate growled.

"Ok fellas, kill the shit. Jesus fucking Christ ain't what we here for. Me steerer, what the fuck do you think you are doing allowing us to work dry throated? Do you want to siphon the beer?" the SJ questioned the steerer. "No." the steerer said. "I'm disappointed in you all. Just for a bottle of beer you all wanna slice my throat?"

"Don't give us that shit man, go bring the crate so that we can start guzzling." the 1st shipmate responded. Finaly the steerer was fed up. He had no choice but to produce the crate of beer.

For want of a better person to make a job perfect, Aisosa a Buccaneer, had no choice but to use Idaami a Maphite to complete his job. Although they have known each other for a long time, they were still as close as water and oil put together.

They attended the same primary school, University of Benin Staff School, Benin city, the same secondary school, the University of Benin Demonstration Secondary School (UDSS) and finally it happened that they were in the same department in the same university which happened to be the University of Benin. It was Aisosa's job to get the dirty job done like sending a scam format, to his *maga* (victim), through the interernt to convince him why it was in his interest to play football and finally, get him to pay a certain amount of money to a particular bank account which was Idaami's. Idaam's job was to go to the bank and collect the money and for that he gets 30% of the money. It seemed an easy way to make money and he seemed to be enjoying the life the money was affording him. After all, what could be more pleasurable than doing nothing, yet having money in one's pockets for spending? That was for Idaami. For Asisosa he was happy with the kind of life he was leading. He gets women cheap. Of course the ladies don't mind. The economic situation in the country is so bad that if a student can afford a car while in school, they see the person as a star, if that person can give them a free ride to school or any place especially if they get to be in the front seat, that person has given them the world and for that they are willing to sleep with him. Aisosa had a Toyota Camry 2.0 with a factory fitted AC which he puts on whenever he wants to impress a new catch. But that was the least of his excitement. With the money he got, was able to block those courses blockable without sweat; and for the ones not *blockable*, he reads

for them. Somehow he managed to balance his activities together with his academics. In his opinion, there's no doubt
that money scammed is twice as sweet as money earned. But
such is the force cyber fraud has over its practitioners. The
moment one gets in, it is difficult to pull out. The game is
really sweet especially if you get to see the reward. Of course,
it doesn't matter if the person duped has committed suicide.
Money is always welcomed whether in a dirty sack or not.

Desmond was relaxing listening to *Break Away* by Kelly
Clerkson. The song inspires him very much. He had just
come from school. He wanted something to relax his nerves.
He was meditating on the song. He came to realize that female rock artistes inspires him more compared to male ones.
He saw rock as a masculine thing and when females venture
into it, he always appreciated them and then he would ask
himself the question: *if women can do this why can't I?* …not
necessarily music but anything he can do with his life that
wound continue to live after his death. He had a vision of
being great but somehow there were obstacles to his becoming great. He wondered again. *Why do people say rock songs is
of the devil,* if there is anything rock songs does for him, it
was to challenge him to accomplish his dreams, to meditate
on life which is good if one wants progress. It is just like
marijuana people condemned. For some people, Marijuana
draws them closer to God; it draws them into another realm
where they can clearly see the good attributes of God and
his mercies on their lives. And now that he's listening to this
song, he was thinking about his life he knew he had the ba-
sic ingredients of becoming great which was a great internal

energy concentration and perservance. But the problem with him was, his vices got the better part of him. His major vice was womanizing. He cannot deny himself that pleasure: that ultimate pleasure of stripping a woman naked and entering her. He knew he had to suppress his desire for the opposite sex but then not now perhaps when he gets married. He felt pity for those great men women had brought down. It is true money can save one from everything except a beautiful woman. Sometimes when he thinks of the the issue he feels helpless, but he also thinks that women were created for admiration. Why should one fail to admire that beautiful lady passing by in the street?

His mind again roamed to dwell on the issue at hand. He'd been getting this pressure from his rugged brothers on how to even the score with the Axemen and Bird Boys. Each time he thought about it, the thought of Ivie paralysed his mind to think straight. In other to clear his mind, he decided to take a stroll around the neighborhood. He hadn't walked more than five blocks when he heard an uproar. Tracing where it was coming from, he discovered it was the next two houses. Getting there, he asked, "What is happening?"

"The girl over there" a witness pointed his finger to her direction, "is owing her friend five grand and it seems she couldn't pay; so her friend asked some guys to do her the favour of shaking the girl down to see if any thing would come out of her but it seems she's really broke. When the guys saw nothing was coming out, they got frustrated and hit her. I guess that was the scream that got you here." the guy explained.

"So you are saying for a measly five grand she's being

given the treatment?"

"Yeah! If you can call five grand measly." the guy responded

There are times when Desmond forgets he is in a school environment; that at such times it could be very rough for students. Aside his parents being rich, Desmond was the big eye of the Buccaneer's Confraternity, a confraternity for the rich. It is unfortunate that some really bright students, because of lack of money, are not able to make it to the Buccaneer's ship. They end up becoming a Bird or an Axe.

Desmond walked up to the two guys shaking her down. He knew they must be frat men, probably Bird or Axe. They do this kind of thing all the time. He had learned out of other peoples experience that it is best to stay out of cases like this especially when it involves a beautiful lady. And the lady they were shaking down was more than handsome but less than beautiful. The bottom line: she was kissable. In a polite manner, he said to them, "I understand that this lady here is owing you five grand."

"Yes." one of them said

"But na who you be? How this matter take affect you?"

"My chairman, I really don't know her per se, but we are in the same department

Though I doubt if she knows me".

"So?" one of them asked.

"I 'm assuring you guys that if you can come this time tomorrow, you'll get your money. Please just leave her alone."

The two of them looked at each other then looked at Desmond.

"Bros wetin make us come tomorrow and we no find the

money, na she go suffer am."

They made a show of hitting her again but didn't and said "You get luck. If not because of your guardian angel you for cry blood today." And they left.

Desmond didn't know why he had to do this, maybe he didn't like to see a man hit a woman or lady in distress or perhaps it is just the natural inclination in men to protect the weak and helpless especially beautiful women. Nonetheless, he said to her; "Stop crying cutie, everything is gonna be ok." At that point the little crowd that had gathered started to disperse. "Look, tomorrow we are going to give them the money and they won't disturb you again ok?"

She nodded her head. She didn't know what to say.

He gave her his hand which she collected and he drew her up.

"Have you eaten anything today?" she nodded her head again. She didn't want to be romantically involved with this Mr. nice guy. Often time they end up to be more trouble than they are worth. She wanted to be miles away from him as much as she can.

"Where is your room?" Desmond asked. She led him to her room but when they got to the door, Desmond said: "Ok I just want to know so that by the time I"ll come tomorrow, I won't be knocking on some other person's door. Sure you're gonna be okay?" She nodded her head again. This time Desmond had to smile "Ok, tomorrow then."

She nodded her head, Desmond looked at her for one last time then left.

The next day, as he had promised he came around 12:00hrs although the guys were expected around 14:00hrs he wanted to make sure she was not given the treatment again. He knocked on her door and she opened.

"Hey you are early, this guys are not expected until 2pm" she said

"I didn't know you can talk. Yesterday you barely said a word."

"Come on, you saw what happened, yeaterday I was not in the mood after what happened."

"Talking about what happened what really happened?" Desmond asked.

"Hmm, I…I would really not like to talk about it."

"Ok, if that's how you feel about it. Well, you are ok right?"

"Yea."

I was passing by when the shit was going on. I don't like to see ladies especially a beautiful lady like you in distres. I just don't like it. She didn't want them to go into the subject *beauties in distres*. So she said; "Did you…emm, did you bring the money?"

"Yeah! Five grand right?" he drew the money out of his pocket and gave it to her. But she was reluctant to collect the money but Desmond made her collect it.

"How long are you giving me to pay you?" she asked.

"C'mon for this there's no string attached. You just pay them and get on with your life,ok?"

She became relaxed a little bit.

"Are you saying you don't want the money back?" In another two weeks time I will get the money."

"Look, let's not complicate things, ok? I don't want the money back and like I said before there's no string attached."

She was relaxed totally now. "While waiting for them, let me make potato chips, you are gonna like it. It's the least I can do to say thank you."

"By all means, do whatever you need to do baby." She was a rock fan too and so before she went into the kitchen, she inserted Avril Lavigne CD into her DVD player. When she was gone, Desmond realized he had not taken a good look at the room. He saw that a 14 inch Samsumg television was stached in a corner of the room, beside it was a LG DVD player with its speakers scattered all over the room. A storage cart beside her bed was stocked with all kinds of beverages like average size powdered milk, average size chocolate beverage, a packet of cubed sugar, a cup of butter, a cup of Mayonnaise, a bottle of honey a bottle of groundnut, two cartons of corn flakes about five or six tins of sardine. There were more but he really didn't want to bother himself to see those things. Her bed, 18 inches was neatly arranged. The teddy bears on it that he thought were two were actually four. A framed picture of dogs smoking cigarette and playing cards was hung on one side of the walls. The colour of the drapes which was green matched the colour of her bed spread and the colour of rug carpet on the floor. The bottom line, she had style. It was a self contained apartment. One door beside it was leading to the WC and bath together. She came out of the door leading to the kitchen. Desmond said; "Didn't know you are a rock fan. Avril Lavigne is one of my best rock artistes. I like the way she expresses herself in her songs and talking about expressions, I like your apartment; it's so nice and homely. If Architecture departmennt were to be in this school, I would have assumed that's what you are studying. So what are you into?"

"Botany." she replied.

"What level?"

"Third year."

"I see. You really have gotten yourself a nice apartment"

"Thank you. In another five minutes the chips will be ready. So what department are you?"

"Production Engineering."

"What level?"

"I'm in my finals now."

"Hmmm, so who is your 12 unit course?"

"Sorry?"

"Oh, don't give me that. You finalist don't take relationships serious. You just find a girl you can use for the remaining of your stay in school and dump her when you grad."

Desmond was blushing. "That's not exactly true." he said. Before he could continue, she said; "A moment please." and she went into the kitchen. Before she would come out, there was a knock on the door. She came out of the kitchen to answer it.

When she opened the door it was the two guys harassing her the day before

Their faces were like stone but she was not terrified. One of them said

"The money?"

She went inside collected the money and gave it to them. They counted the money, when they discovered it was correct, they gave her one last look, nodded and left without another word. When she closed the door, Desmond asked, "Who was it?"

"The guys of yesterday." she replied.

"It is just 1 pm and they are not expected until 2pm. Thank God we prepared for it."

She looked at him for about 10 seconds then went into the kitchen. When she came out she was holding a tray with potato chips and a bowl of egg sauce. She left it gently on the table, went back into the kitchen again and brought out two bottled water and two glass cups from the fridge and took it to the room. They sat opposite each other with the tray of food in between them. During the meals, Desmond asked: "I don't understand, do they teach you how to cook in botany?"

"What?"

"My heaven! This is delicious."

Desmond couldn't be sure but he thought he saw her smile. It seemed it came and disappeared without a trace. She said "thank you." Desmond couldn't understand if it were to be other girls, they would have been dying to kiss him but this girl in front of him didn't careless if he is Leonado di'Caprio or not . He realized he didn't know her name. "I'm sorry, what did you say the name is again?"

"What do you mean again? I have not told you before."

"Don't mind me, I thought I heard the name before."

"My name is Anita."

"Anita Baker?"

"You can call me Anny my friends call me that

"Honey?"

"Anny." She almost shouted but she was smiling.

"Ok, I get it, you've got a beautiful smile."

"Thank you."

This time she was blushing when she said it.

— 149 —

Desmond suddlenly realized that for the four months, he and Ivie had been dating, Ivie had never cooked for him. They were always going to eatries.

"So what's your name?" Anita asked.

"Desmond."

She nodded her head

"Do you live around here?"

"Some few blocks away." Desmond replied. Finally, the meal was finished. She got up to take away the tray.

"There are still some chips in the kitchen. Do you care for some?"

"Hey hon. I'm thoroughly satisfied. Haven't eaten anything like this for a long time now. I'm really grateful for the meal. Thank you."

"You're welcome."

She took the tray into the kitchen. When she came out, she said, "You're gonna have to excuse me for a moment. The heat in the kitchen made me sweat a little I want to have my bath."

"Emm, I'm afraid, I'll have to leave now."

Come on, it ain't gonna take much time. Let's say about five minutes. It's more like a shower."

"I really would like to stay but there is this lecture I have to attend by 2:30 pm. The lecture is such that if you don't attend it, there is no way in hell you're gonna pass it." She made a face like she was offended then said; "Ok, if you must leave. It is really unfortunate. I was gonna give you a swell time."

"Ok, can we carry it over?" Desmond asked. Desmond was up, going towards the door .She held his hand in a romantic way then said; "Hope I'm gonna see you again. What you did for me, if I'm to have a naira for each time I've come across people like you, I would have three naira."

"Really, I'm flattered. I appreciate that."

"Oh, and again if I want to appreciate, I go to the extremes. If you think telling you I would have three naira for each time I've come across persons like you as appreciation you've got another think coming. See, if there's anything, I mean anything I can do for you don't hesitate ok?"

Desmond was smiling when he asked; "Anything?"

"You bet your ass baby, I'm right here for you." Desmond looked at her again and thought she has got inside beauty and if truth be told she wasn't bad externally. She was wearing a tight blue rugged jeans and a black spaghetti top that cleaved her body making her breast to shoot out in a forceful way. The breast, although average sized seemed a little bigger for her because of the way her spag top was hugging her body so closely. The ass on the other hand was averagely perfect for her. But what Desmond admired most was her model like figure. Skinning to the extent of flexibility in bed but not skinning to the extent that will make her look like an AIDS patient.

Desmond by now was outside her room while she was inside holding the door. He wanted to give her a kiss but he restrained himself. He said; "The Potato chips and eggs sauce you prepared was excellent. What are the chances of eating something like that again this weekend?"

"What day exactly?"

"Sunday."

"You've got yourself a deal."

"Ok then by 5 p.m I should be here."

"Ok, and thanks for being my hero."

"You're welcome." Then he left.

On Saturday before the Sunday he was to see Anita, Desmond called for a MIT with his chiefs. The MIT was slated for 15:00hrs the first to arrive was Charles Owoseni, the 1st shipmate of the deck. He was from Edo State. Before becoming the first shipmate of the deck he was known for his doggedness. Way back when he was a deckhand, because he looked gentle people in his class thought he had no force. So on a certain day a lecturer who doesn't speak out loud asked the class representative to tell the class that in another 10 minutes, he would lecture them. The class, knowning full well that the lecturer doesn't talk loud started struggling to have the front row seat. Charles was no exception. Hardly had Charles settled down when a course mate of his entered the class and told Charles that he was occupying the seat before he left the class and that he needed Charles to stand up. He was newly initiated into the Jurist Confraternity and so he felt like a god. The class knew Charles would not be taken for such a ride. Of course Charles gave the guy a deaf ear. To cut the long story short, the guy slapped Charles visiously. Every body was surprised, and wondered what *is Charles gonna do now.*

But at that moment the lecturer stepped into the class. The whole drama subsided. After the class, Charles made enquires as to where the guy was living. Thank goodness the guy was living alone. That night about 20:00hrs, Charles took with him two other Lords and went to Obinna's house (The guy's name was Obinna.) Getting there, they wore their mask and knocked. 'He Lives in Him' by Diana Ross was playing inside. It seemed the guy was enjoying himself. When he opened the door he saw three guys in a black mask. Thinking it was some of his friends playing some kind of prank. He said "Hey what is this suppose to ......? But he wasn't allowed to complete the question. Charles was the first to hit him. He kicked him violently in the stomach which sent him sprawling on the floor. They quickly entered. One of them closed the door.

While the other two was kicking Obinna furiously, the third guy quickly increased the volume of the song playing because Obinna was shouting for help. When they were tired of that they brought out a piece of cloth arranged in form of a sling with stone in one end and started hitting him. After about 15 minutes doing this, Charles brought out a penknife and asked the other two to strap his right hand to a wooden stool in the room. Already, Obinna was slipping into unconsciousness. He didn't care what they were going to do with his hand. What happened next brought him out of unconciousness. Charles, with all his force, stabbed Obinna's palm in the middle. The knife went through the palm and went half way through the top of the stool. Obinna was at sea of what expression to let out. Much to his shock, he couldn't scream. As a matter of fact he didn't feel much pain. Little did he know that a world of pain was awaiting him. The real pain would be felt when the knife is removed. The music was stopped, then they left the house leaving him like that in the hope that some Good Samaritan would come to his aid. The next day, nobody knew how it spread around but it seemed the whole school knew what happened to Obinna. Everybody was asking everybody, *have you seen Obinna recently?* In the

University teaching Hospital he was rushed to, it was said, it'll take another 3-4 months before the hand can get healed.

What that meant is that Obinna would miss his forth coming exams which invariably would lead to extention. Charles got a new form of respect that was not shown him before. The second to arrive was Adebisi Adebayo. The steerer of the deck, He was from Lagos State. Before becoming the streerer of the deck, he was holding the postion of the 2nd shipmate. But for him, the lack of respect from the Axemen would have gone unpunished. In Ekosodi, a locality owend by the Axemen was a place other frat men were wary of living. It was the kind of place where one sleeps with one eye close and the other open. The Axemen there have been agitating that they were not getting enough respect from the other confraternities considering that Edo State was their mother land. In other to set the record straight, they decided to make a member of one the confraternities a scape goat as a lesson for others. Unfortunately a Buccaneer was picked as the scape goat. He was bloodied mercilessly and placed at the village's gate where all could see the scape goat while going to school in the morning. A low profile Buccaneer living in Ekosodi saw this and the note on him that said: 'Henceforth, all other frat guys should show some respect to any Axemen in this campus or else..." that was the message. The low profile Buccaneer quickly arranged for the bloodied Buccaneer to be taken to a nearby clinic. Immediately he informed the house. Unfortunately, the big eye and the KMS were not around. There was confusion as to what to do, should they wait for the B.E to come before taking any action or should they act immediately? Majority of the house said they should wait. But the 2nd shipmate (ABC steerer) would not have it. That evening, an Axeman living in Osasogie, an area controlled by the Buccaneers was abducted by the 2nd shipmate and his crew. He was bloodied but his was worse considering the broken bones in his fingers. He was also placed at Ekosodi's gate early in the morning with a message written on a piece of paper that if anything so much as a scratch is found in any Buccaneer's body, a bloodied Axeman would be the least of their troubles. Of course the Axemen knew better than to hit back. The incident earned the Buccaneer another level of respect in the campus. The third to arrive was Theodore Onome popularly called Theodore Bagwell by Lords. He was the KMS of the deck. He was 6ft 1 inch tall, had a muscular body that made him huge, dark complexioned, with a face like that of pinnochio with a long nose. His eyebrows were so thick it became necessary to shave every now and then. His eyes almost at the sides of his face was something that gave people a pause when they see him for the first time. His friends popularly joked that if the devil had had a name it would have been Theodore Onome.

Although the Buccaneers frown at people like this, there were times when it becomes necessary to lobby such people to their side. Seeing him alone gave one the creeps. Talking with him frightens the hell out of you. There are some seeing him for the first time thinks the devil had been made flesh. Theodore in his small life time had seen better days. In and out of jail, stab wounds all over his body from fights with other frats men and stubborn lubbers as well. It is true that what propels a man to fight is fear and hate. While some hate

U. V. ERNEST

Theodore, others fear him. And so for one reason or the other they were always trying to bring him down. How he had managed to keep himself alive was a miracle. At one time a girl in his class who was popularly called *the radio station* because she was so easy to pick up and if truth be told she had seen more ceilings than Michael Angelo, was being pestered by some lubbers in the class. These men knowing she was the easy type wanted an easy lay. But they were surprised that she was difficult to get. She, on the other hand, knew what they wanted but over time she made herself classy. Though she isn't that beautiful or handsome but she's got the curves. The moment one sees her one can't help but think of figure 8.

All she wanted from them was the proper thing a gentlemen should do which was, to take her out and give her a treat and for that, she would be theirs. But these guys were so poor, the desert rat was richer than them. They didn't want to spend a dime yet they wanted to enjoy her intimately. When the pestering became too much to the extent she was being threatened by them, she went to Theodore.

Theodore too, has gotten his share of sex from her. She liked Theodore a lot maybe because of the gentleness and care Theodore showered her. She wanted a long term relationship but Theodore wasn't the type to nurse a relationship so they ended it at that but remained friends. When she fingered the two boys that were pestering her life, Theodore went to the two boys and said: "My girlfriend told me you two guys have been disturbing her. Is that true?"

The two guys looked at each other then at him. They were just some few inches taller than Theodore's waist and so looking at him they had to lift their head to an angle before they could see his face. They were already as nervous as a turkey at Christmas. They took a step backward. "We... no, no, no...," they started saying, "There must be some kind of mistake somewhere."

One of them turned to the other and said; "We are her best friends right?" The other nodded his head. "We just wanna watch out for her right?" The other nodded his head again. "It seems so many boys are disturbing her these days. Frankly, we don't want anything from her." He turned to the other again and said,"We were going to buy her five thousand naira worth of gift for her birthday coming up soon right?" The other looked at Theodore then at his friend again and nodded his head. The guy doing the talking loked at Theodore and said: "Hey Bro, we just want the best for her, nothing more."

"Ok," Theodore said "I want you to get this straight into your fucking heads, the next time she complains to me that you guys so much as give her a passing glance or a call to say hello, trust me, having a broken rib would be the least of your worries. Do you understand?"

The guy doing the talking asked his friend again "We understand him perfectly well right?" The other guy nodded his head again.

"By the way," Theodore continued "Since when has the school employed other students to bodyguard students?"

"We only want to be her friend nothing more." He turned to the other guy "Ain't that right?" The other guy nodded his head. "Ok fellas, let's get this straight, you're not to remain friends with my girlfriend because in the place I grew up there's only one reason boys become friends with girls.

I just wanna make sure that doesn't happen, understand?" Theodore warned.

"That ain't gonna happen right?" The guy doing the talking asked his friend again. The friend nodded as usual.

"About the birthday gift where is the money?" Theodore asked. Immediately the question was asked the countenance of the two guys changed. The other that had been nodding looked like he was going to piss in his pant. He looked at his friend doing the talking to bail them out of this. The guy doing the talking said "Hmm...hmm...hmm..."

"Hmm what?" Theodore barked.

"Hmm, actually, we were going to see if the bank could lend us some money." he turned to his friend "That is what we were going to do, right?" The friend looked at Theodore half way up the face then nodded.

"You fucking bastard, you don't have money yet you want to lay a girl, it doesn't work out that way in this school. Now get the fuck outta here."

They started to turn to run with speed when they heard, "hey! Come back here." from Thodore. They turned to face him again. Theodore said, "Your friend here he is not dumb right?" the guy doing the talking in turn asked his friend, "You piece of shit, are you dumb?"

The friend was at sea of what to say. He didn't know what to do. But somehow he managed to nod and shake his head at the same time. Theodore couldn't help it any longer, he turned and laughed.

A week later the girl came to thank him for the favour. She made it known that Theodore can always have her if he's in the mood.

Soon, word got out that she's Theodore's girlfriend but the consequence was that she started loosing customers.

The fouth DM to arrive was the 2nd shipmate of the deck. His name was Olatunde Oyebanjo. He was dark complexioned, 5ft 6in tall with a small face. His hands and feet were small too. He had small eyes, medium sized nose and a small mouth. He was popularly known as the 'Chinese kid' because of these features. It started right from primary school but somehow the name managed to stick so that even in the University, he was still known as the 'Chinese kid'.

What the 1st shipmate is to the big eye, the 2nd shipmate is to the steerer. For that reason it is important that the 2nd shipmate hails from Lagos just like the steerer. When the ABC steerer was the 2nd shipmate, Olatunde was among the members of the crew that abducted the akite and had him bloodied. The ferocity with which Olatunde, who was still a deckhand bloodied the bloody akite, convinced Adebisi the ABC steerer and XY 2nd shipmate that Olatunde was a material. And so when the big eye appointed him the steerer of the deck, he quickly made it known that Olatunde was the person he wants as his 2nd shipmate.

The fifth to arrive was Uchenna Issac. He was the Hauler of the deck. What the EFCC was to Obasanjo during his administration, the hauler was to the big eye. His job was to haul erring Lords who were going off course. In buccaneering, discipline matters a lot. The Lord who chooses to be undisciplined will only have himself to blame. By virtue of his job, he was expected to be huge. Isaac hailed from Imo State. He was 6ft 3ins tall muscular and well built, fair complexioned handsome in a way that was irresistible to women especially as he was tall. A number of modeling outfits had approached him but he had always turned them down for one reason or the other. Perhaps he didn't want anything to get in the way of his studies. Most times it's just him alone the FF carries along if he wants to dive lagging Lords who haven't paid their dues. Behind the handsome face of an angel was a devilish mind operating in disguise. He was the 1st shipmate of the XYZ Big eye before he graduated. Aside being the 1st shipmate for the XYZ big eye, he was also the hatchet man for the big eye. Most times when the big eye of the tenure wants to float an idea to the house and he knows the idea will be opposed, he uses his 1st shipmate to do the job. The 1st shipmate who was Uchenna Isaac as at the last tenure, floated the idea and somehow made it stick. Although in the the end he was hated by the house nonetheless his job had been carried out. He was also like a special adviser to the big eye. And in most cases the bigeyeship was usually anchored to the 1st shipmate because of their special role as advisers and hatchet man for the big eye. But in the case of Uchanna Isaac, a special quality was missing that hindered him from getting this important position. Nonetheless, he was contented that he was still a deckmaster. Since most Lords do not like him, it was only natural that the ABC big eye made him the hauler of the deck.

The next to arrive was the Sailing Jin named Gabrielle Edobor. The person responsible for the social aspect of buccaneering. He arranges for foods and drinks for Lords and sometimes women. Because of the nature of the job, it became necessary to anchor the position to a ladies' man especially when that person was conversant with the buccaneering sea songs. He was 5' 8" tall with a triangular head. His tummy was almost like that of a 5 months pregnant woman and that was because of beer. His greatest asset was his humorous remarks about things in general. It was this attribute that endeared him to the female folks. Ladies like to be around him because each time they are around him, they cannot help but laugh at most of what he says and in the process some of them fall in love. This was how he got to sleep with up to 30% of the ladies in his world. The last to arrive was the FF. His head was circular with average sized eyes and nose and a big mouth. The neck was like a long bridge connecting his head to the rest of the body. His head to his waist was longer than from his waist to his feet. He's got the dress sence of *Will Smith*. Whenever he goes for classes, the ladies and even some guys turned to look at him the second time. One of the reasons he was respected was because of the money he had. He spent money like a drunken sailor. Like there's no tomorrow. Whenever he took a girl out, that day becomes a memorable day for the girl for a long time to come. Because he was financially rugged, he was made the FF of the deck. The FF's duty was to keep account of the money that comes and goes out of BAN's account. Whenever a charity project was to be carried out, ruggedity demands he provides a huge sum of the money. Not exactly his duty but as a rugged Lord, he does not have to be told.

The meeting was supposed to be outside the house but because the sun was raining outside, they chose to hold it inside. Already there was a crate of beer waiting to be served. The BE cleared his throat and said: "Alora DMs, you are all welcome to this meeting of short notice." As he was saying this, he was passing around chilled bottles of Star beer to the DMs. "As I'm aware," he continued "The 1st JJ went without a hitch. I'm also told that from the look of things, three lubbers won't be able to make ship. I would like to know why." the question was meant for the steerer.

"Alora me big eye, all other protocols observed," The steerer said, "aside that the three lubber have not completed their induction dues, intellectually they are marooned". The Big eye didn't press it further. It was a good enough reason. Although during induction, a lubber was always sacrificed as a tradition. This is to make others more rugged in the adventure. Nonetheless, if it becomes necessary to sacrifice more than one, then more than one was sacrifised in the hope that the few that would make ship would be more rugged to weather the storms of life. The Big eye continued: "What about the preparation for our ST? How many Lords have responded?" The question was directed to the FF. "About 50 Lords have cut their dues for the ST, some said before the week runs out and others say probably next week. The money we have on ground can take care of all the budgets except the souvenir. By the time the remaining Lords cut their dues by next week, we should be fully prepared." The Big eye nodded his head. It seemed everything was going on as planned. He asked again: "Has the price for the waste bin been confirmed?" The question was directed to the SJ

"I browsed the market the other day and discovered that there were two major types we can use. The basket type and bucket type with some kind of customized cover for the waste bin. No doubt, once seen, one will know it is a waste bin. The basket type is N100.00 for each while the bucket type is N200.00 for each. But there will be discount if we are buying much." the SJ answered.

"Have we tried to find out how many departments and offices we have in this school?" the big eye asked.

"We are still working on it." The steeeer answered.

"Good." the big eye said.

"The major reason I called for this MIT," the big eye continued, is that I want you all to be extraordinarily careful now. I don't want anymore troubles with our black and blue friends (Axemen and Birdboys). All trouble must be avoided at all costs. Our black and blue friends are reducing their guard and that is how I want them to be. I want them to feel safe. I want them to assume we are going to forget our vengeance. Meanwhile I want you all to be observant. Alora KMS, I want you to keep a close watch on the DMs of these fraternities. Certainly you cannot do this alone, I want you all others to join him in this. These things can be done without anybody raising an eyebrow. On no account should their suspicion be raised. Alora K, hope the tools with you are still in good working condition? If not better start cleaning and oiling them. Do we still have enough tools in the house? "

"Yes" the KMS answered. The Big eye continued.

"Hope nobody is having trouble with his departmental course?"

"No." the house echoed.

"What about the deckhands, how are they faring?"

"It seems they are doing well." the steerer answered.

"Of course, it must go without saying that the deckhands must not know about present plans. When the time is ripe for them to know, we'll pass the word. Still, I want you to spread the word that on no account should they get into trouble with any of the confraternities. Their business for now as well as for you is to stay out of trouble. Is there anything that has not been discussed?"

The DMS looked at each other but nobody had anything to say except the streerer who asked; "What about our next JJ?"

"Yeah, lest I forget, the next JJ will be next week Saturday. Alora steerer ensure all our deckhands know of the date. They are to come and observe if anybody is cross carpeting from other fraternities to ours. "Anything else?" It seemed there was nothing more to discuss. The athmosphere became relaxed to enjoy their drinks. After that, the BE bade them SO. They echoed their response and left.

The Big eye couldn't wait for the next day. He wanted desperately to be with Anita. He loved the serenity of the house, the pleasant way she talks, her reserved attitude, the way she smiles even the way she walks. The food was another catalyst that made him fall in love. Although Desmond had promised to go by 5PM, he couldn't help it when he left for her place by 4pm. He wanted to be close to her again. He couldn't understand his feelings. He knew it wasn't too healthy to be feeling that way about a lady. He was nonetheless helpless to do anything about it.

When he knocked at her door, he secretly hoped she won't be at home so that he could go and come back by 5pm. He was about to knock again when he saw the door handle turned and the door was opened. Seeing her standing in front of him got him mesmerized. He couldn't believe what he was seeing; she was in bumsters and netted spaghetti top that made it possible to see her nipples from a close distance. Desmond was unaware that he was staring at the nipples until she coughed to get his attention. "Hey handsome, are you going to stand out there or you are going to come inside?"

"Oh! I'm terribly sorry, how long have I been unconscious?"

"Almost like five minutes."

"What! You're not kidding, are you? Damn! You know, I'm really sorry; you've got these great legs. I've never seen anything like them before. Your mom must have done a great job bringing you up."

"Don't play smart with me; I saw the angle of your eyes. From the angle your eyes, you couldn't possibly have noticed the legs. They were focused on my chest."

"Ow! Was it that obvious?"

"You are not a good liar."

Anita was the epitome of African beauty. She had poise, she walked elegantly, she talked smoothly, and she's got the average height of 5'7', chocolate in complexion, handsome in a way that attracted more attention. She had that killing figure and somehow, she knew how to make a man relax. Desmonds had to shift a doll on the bed before he could sit. *Pretty Woman* was on the screen. Desmond asked "Are you from the old school, who is still watching *Pretty Woman* these days?"

"If you have not been watching, start now."

"What good will that do?"

"At least, you can learn how to woo a woman."

"Hey Anny, that last…"

" Hold on a moment please," Anny went into the kitchen, and then came out with a bottle of ice water and a glass cup.

"Like I was gonna say, the last few days, you've been running through my head, worse is, at nights, I can't sleep. Ain't these legs of yours tired of running?"

"What's that supposed to mean, a standard pickup line you've been using to woo ladies on campus? It ain't gonna work for me and moreover is that why you couldn't wait till 5 P.M before coming?"

"'Now you know I'm not making it up. At least that's proof."

"It doesn't prove anything," she said "Now that I've not prepard anything, what are you going to eat?"

"Are you kidding me? Seeing you alone is food enough; especially when you are dressed up like this. No doubt I can eat you alive. You know, you seem to have added another meaning to the word 'EDIBLE' you look sumptious baby."

"You guys are all the same, *all foam no beer*." She got up from where she was sitting and went to the storage cart and brought out a bottle of groundnut that had barely been eaten; she took it to him, opened it and poured some in a saucer for both of them. She went to the fridge in the kitchen and brought out a 1 litre carton of orange juice and brought it to him. She carried a glass cup for both of them. While the film was going on, they were picking groundnuts from the saucer and chewing. Every now and then, they would gulp down some quantity of juice to clean up their throats. Not much was said during this but it was not to say they weren't feeling good. After sometime, Desmond called, "Anny!"

"Yeah?"

"Do you think oral sex is wrong for married couples?"

"You mean using the mouth and tongue to stimulate the

genitals?"

"Yeah." Desmond answered. "Well, I think it is somewhere in the Bible where it is written, a man should not deny his wife his body; likewise the woman and that they should explore their bodies to the fullest."

"Are you sure? Can you remember the exact chapter?"

"What am I, a pastor?"

"You and I both know you won't make a good pastor. Anyway, the way you sounded you seem so positive."

"Yeah, I'm positive."

"What about unmarried couples, what do you think?"

"What the fuck do you mean? Of course it is wrong or are you a Muslim? Even in Islam it is wrong. So don't even go there."

"Have you tasted of the pleasure?"

"Why, yes, about the sweetest thing you can think of."

"What's your opinion about it for the unmarried?"

"My opinion doesn't count but between you and me, we both know it is bad."

"What the hell, we are in the 21st century. You cannot deprive youths from going into adventure. Even teenagers want to see for themselves. That's the world we are living in. It's so fucked up. Did you hear the story of that guy that got his dick bitten off?"

"Damn! What happened?"

"Mygosh! you mean all you do in this school is read book?"

"You wouldn't know." Desmond answered cautiously.

"This guy had this new catch he mounted to his place. Soon they were in the act. She started sucking him. The guy was in cloud nine. He seemed he saw Jesus, he started calling his name *Jesus, Jesus*... out of pleasure. Little did he know that the girl was an epileptic patient? Soon, from calling Jesus out of pleasure he started calling him for rescue. But it was too late and moreover Jesus don't save people like that. The girl, during the sucking got her attack again. Unfortunately the only thing in her mouth was the boy's dick, she had no choice. She bit off his dick. That was how the boy got himself killed."

"Wow, what a hell of a story, that's one horrible way to die." Desmond responded. At that moment the film ended. It was 18:05hrs. Anita got up to remove the film and in place of that she slotted in one of her Mariah Carey's albums. With the sun being swallowed up by the earth the room became dark. She put on one of the colored bulbs to make the air in her room romantic. With the talk of oral sex and the pleasure in it, she found herself in the mood so she said, "Hey Handsome, do you think you can do me a little favour?"

"Depends."

"I have been having this pain in my back, do you think you can help me massage it?

"My pleasure." Desmond answered. She lay flat on the bed with her back to the ceiling. Desmond, in other to be in a better position to message her properly, climbed her back so that his ass was a little below her ass. From that point, his hand can get to any part of her back with ease. He started massaging her shoulder down to her waist and back to the shoulder but it seemed her netted spaghetti top was making her uncomfortable so she asked Desmond to help her raise her spagetti top to her shoulder so that she could get a better feel at the massaging. Desmond obliged. He did as he was told. With the sight of smooth chocolate skin, his dick began to feel excited, his stock began to grow. After a minute or so of massaging her, he bent to kiss her back. She's been in the mood for so long, she was waiting for him to make the first move. She asked him to get up but Desmond thought he had offended her by kissing her back so he started saying; "I'm sorry I'm sorry," But when he got up, and she turned so that her back was on the bed, he was surprised that she was smiling. He also noticed that her boobs were a little bigger and her nipples seemed to be forcing their way out of the netted spag. She raised her hand a little bit and used her index finger to signal him to come. That was when Desmond smiled. He went over to her again climbed her crotch, bent down to kiss her on the mouth. He couldn't get his fill of her mouth and tongue. It seemed their tongues were fighting each other. Her lips tasted of something he couldn't place his mind on. It was so sweet a sensation, they were in the act for like five minutes when she started undressing him, while that was going on, his hand was inside her netted spaghetti top caressing her boobs, soon it became clear the net was hindering his access to her boobs. At that point he raised himself up so that he could strip off the shirt he was putting on. While doing that, she was also taking off her blouse; it seemed it was a competition: they both removed their tops at the same time. They smiled at each other. Then Desmond bent down to start the season two of the kissing. While he was kissing her, he was fondling one of her boobs with one of his hands. Her whole body seemed to be wriggling with pleasure. She was in a state of euphoria. She didn't even know when she started

struggling with the belt on his trousers. The unstrapping of
the belt seemed to be done unconsciously. She couldn't wait
to have his dick in her hand, by that time, she was getting
wet. Desmond on the other hand was trying to unfasten the
button on her bumster but without success. She observed
the difficulty he was having so she helped him. He returned
his concentration on the boobs again. It looked like a play
thing for him. He caressed and sucked the nipples; using
his tongue to stimulate the tip of her nipples one after the
other. She went back to her former assignment of getting to
fondle his dick. She unzipped him. It seemed his jean had
been doing a great job of concealing the growth of his stock.
When the pair of trousers were down, his dick was bigger
than she had expected. She drew his boxers down and started
fonding his dick and scrotum. While that was going on, his
hands were probing down her pube. The bumsters made it
difficult for him to probe any further. He really didn't want
to leave the boobs but he had no choice. He left the boobs
to tackle the bumster with difficulty. When she was stripped
off the bumsters, Desmond enjoyed the sight he was seeing.
He went back to the boobs again but this time he positioned
himself so that while tickling her nipples with his tongue, a
finger of his was inside her cunt stimulating her clitoris. The
excitement made her body tremble. When the excitement
became too much for her, she got up to position herself to
suck his dick but at that point Desmond was alarmed. He
said, "Wait, wait, wait, you wouldn't by any chance be an epileptic patient would you?"

"Don't be ridiculous, if I am, would I tell you?"

Desmond gave up. He had come this far he wouldn't

allow anything to spoil the mood (unfortunately pussy rules). Desmond relaxed. He laid his back on the bed, she bent over him, held his dick and started sucking him. Desmond was lost in pleasure. His countenance was *the world can go to hell for all he cares.* Out of the pleasure, he smiled, a little smile just for himself alone. After what looked like five minutes of enjoying the pleasure, he got up, went to his wallet and brought out a condom. He slipped it on. He went to her, made her adopt the dog's position and he penetrated her from behind.

When he was tired of that position, he adopted two other different styles before he finally came. The gloves he was putting on didn't make him come early but when finally the show was over, he lay on the bed exhausted. He began to think of the sex. He was trying to judge between her and Ivie. "Hey handsome, "Anita broke his line of thought." That was lovely, I had a great time. Did you?"

"The best time I've ever had." Desmond replied. They were naked and they seem to enjoy themselves naked. She got up naked and went into the kitchen to get a bottle of cold water for them both. It was 18:55hrs and Desmond had no desire of going home. The Mariah Carey album that was playing got to the end and that was when Desmond heard his phone ringing. He got up went to his trouser and removed the phone from the pocket. He discovered his KMS has been calling him for close to 30 minutes. He knew there must be trouble. He took the call.

"Alora me K, what's the trouble?"

"Alora me big eye, A Lord has been blooded by a Maphite, we don't know if he is going to make it alive." The KMS replied.

Chapter 9

Long after other sins were old, avarice remained young. It is also a well known fact that the fish is killed by its open mouth.

For some time now, Idaami had been wanting a bigger percentage from Aisosa. His reason was that his job had more risk compared to that of Aisosa. The Economic and Financial Crime Commission (EFCC) of Nigeria was closing in on cyber fraud practitioners. And the people at risk were the ones going to collect the money from the banks. Some of Idaami's friends in the game had been caught making Idaami to wise up. He explained everything to Aisosa who was also aware of the intricacies and demanded that his percentage be raised to fifty percent. Out of respect for the fact that Idaami was also into game, Aisosa said cautiously, "This is outrageous; don't be naïve. You know as well as I do that in this game, it is necessary you put in some money to convince the *Maga* (victim) in other for them to pay. I bring that money from my own pocket without any assistance from you or anybody else. If we are to go by what you are saying, that means you would be collecting more money than I do.

Just think about it and be reasonable."

"Ok, the least I can come down to is 45 percent."

"45 percent is way too much. Although I'll be doing my self injustice if I give you 35 percent but I can still live with myself. That's the most I can do. What do you say?"

Idaami acted like he was doing some thinking but then he said, "The risk is too much. I'm sorry I can't go below 45 percent."

Aisosa came to the conclusion that it was over between them. That he would have to look for somebody else to do the job Idaami was doing for him. But he had a job at hand that was getting close to climax. He'd need Idaami for one last job.

"Look bro, I know how it is but I want you to do me this favour. There's a job I'm handling now it'll soon climax. I've invested too much in it to let it go down the drain I'll give you 35 percent for this and after now we'll negotiate the percentage you are to collect for subsequent jobs." Aisosa said. Idaami considered it then accepted

Unknown to Aisosa, Idaami's crew had been pressing for a bigger percentage so when Idaami accepted the deal for this last job. He made it clear to his crew that this is the last time he would accept such a percentage. His crew agreed. Three days later, they were together again drinking beer and smoking cigarettes in a pub. They hadn't spent 30 minutes when Idaami's phone rang, it was from Aisosa. He accepted the call. He was given payment detail of the money that had just been credited into his account. The total money was 10,000 pounds which when converted to Nigeria currencies becomes N2, 300,000.00. Thirty five 35 percent of this money amounted to N805,000.00. When Idaami did the calculation, he discovered that 805,000.00 naira would be his for the taking. He was excited when he told his crew of the take. One of them said, do the calculation using 50 percent. Idaami did as was told and he discovered he would have been raking the sum of N 1,150,000.00. He immediately thought of what he would do with such an amount. The glory and prestige that would come. His friends were watching and waiting for him to give them the answer. When finally he raised his head, his grin was from ear to ear. He told them the amount and they nodded their head. The guy who asked him to do the calculation using 50 percent said again: "This is what you are to do, since you are to collect the money, take your 50 percent and give him his 50 percent or will he be coming to the bank to collect his money?"

"Yes of course, that is how we've been doing it. But he is not going to accept that." Idaami replied.

"That is what we are going to give him and that is what he is going to accept."

"It could result to war." Idammi responded. "Those mother fuckers ain't got balls. You saw how it ended between them and the Axemen and even those riff-raff, who call themselves Bird Boys; without them doing anything about it and what is more, those two confraternities hold us in dread. You don't have to worry about anything, we'll be here with you to make sure he doesn't get any ideas." It ended at that.

At the bank, Idaami and his crew, three of them were waiting patiently for Aisosa. They had collected the money without any fuss. The cashier seemed delighted to give Idaami the money. Although back stage, there's a percentage which Idammi gives the cashier and all those involved in ensuring the loot was safe for taking. It was one of the reasons Idammi had to increase the percentage he collects from Aisosa. Idaami figured it was his business to have that angle smoothened so that the angle would not be the fly in the ointment. Finally, Aisosa came. He was told his share of the money by Idaami. They went to the back of the bank. "Is this some kind of a joke?" Aisosa sked.

"I've told you before of the risk involved in this business. Aside that, there are other percentages I give to some of the bankers to make the operation run smoothly. Giving them that leaves me a small lump compared to what you are taking. The 50-50 wil be the deal from now on."

"Who the fuck are you to give me this crap? I call the shots not you". Aisosa said in a measured tone of anger.

One of the boys behind Idaami stepped forward and said: "The rules have changed now brother. It is either you take it or leave it."

"Who the fucking hell are all these guys, how have they enterd the equation?"

"You watch your language bro. We ain't pussies to be pushed around. We are his brothers. You dig?" Another of the boys said raising his voice a little more than necessary.

Of course Aisosa knew who they were. He doesn't have to consult an oracle to know that they are Maphites. He looked at them one after the other. He figured that *half a loaf is better than none.* So he said, "Ok, I agree. Have you transfred the half to my account?"

"I'll do that now. We still have like 30 minutes before the bank closes."

"Ok, good", Aisosa responded. He smiled wolfishly when he shook hands with them before he left. Later that day an alert was sent to his phone that a sum of 1, 150,000.00 naira has been sent to his account.

Three days later Idaami was in his favourite bar close to his house drinking beer. He had called his friends to join him up and they had said they were coming. He lit up his second cigarette thinking of the good life easy money can afford him. *This is the kind of life for me* he thought. The lazying kind of life where he gets to screw the kind of girls he dreams about, not scared to buy beer no matter how many bottles for himself and friends, block his courses no matter the price the lecturer calls, Suddenly, he felt like a bird so free.

A sharp white Benz 190 parked close to the bar. Idammi thought his friends must have gotten themselves a new car from the rackets they are pulling. He was surprised to find Aisosa and two of his friends pull out of the car with the driver still sitting on the driver's seat. When they got to the bar, Idaami was smiling when he said, "What a coincidence, I just got here a few minutes ago. I didn't know you come here too, where is the bar man, let him bring some drinks."

"You fucking bastard," Aisosa responded "There's no such thing as coincidence."

Immediately three shots were left on his chest while one was left on his head. There was no chance of survival, Idaami died instantly. While they were leaving Idaami's friend were coming. They didn't know the other two but they were able to recognize Aisosa. Three days later, a hit was put out on Aisosa by the Maphites. That was the day the KMS called his Big eye to signal him.

"Now that we know what really happened let's wait to know where the wind is blowing before taking any action. The Big eye was addressing his fellow deck masters as a well as the deckhands. They were conducting the 2nd JJ (jaw-jaw) for their lubbers *The Promised Land Hotel* in the government residential area (GRA) in Benin City. Jaw-Jaw (JJ), a word gotten from the word 'jaw'. The traditional JJ is conducted in a beach or island and most times at nights. That was the early days of the confraternity. But soon they metamophosized into a legitimate confraternity were they they don't have to hide or do their things in secret. In the early 80s they were registered as the Buccaneers Association of Nigeria (BAN). They no longer have to do their things in secret making them look like secret cult. They were formally registered with the Nigeria Federal Ministry of Internal affairs and given a registration number. But old habits die hard they say. So instead of them to do their things openly, they clung to the old ways of doing things. In the 90's when violence in Nigeria campuses was getting out of control, the Buccaneers and Pyrates were threatened that their registration would be revoked. That was when the Buccaneers changed phase and decided to use the name 'Brothers across Nigeria' (BAN) for security reasons and to remain afloat legitimately. That was when they got tired of doing their things in secret and started embracing light and doing their things in the open. And so while other confraternities were doing their things in the dark, the Buccaneers and Pyrates openly carried out their functions. So while they were in the hotel preparing their lubbers, Aisosa's crew were agitating that they want to roll to square the debt. That they cannot wait any longer. That they will roll no matter the cost. Meanwhile, the lubbers were packed like sardines in a room, some were already as nervous as a turkey at Christmas. They knew what was in store for them. Jaw-jaw which was gotten from the word jaw, informally, meant at length and formally it meant the grinding grasping or destructive power of something. It became Buccaneers formal way of grinding their lubbers at length. That was why traditionally it was done overnight. Starting from 11p.m to 5 am but for the sake of legitimacy it is now carried out during the day. Over to the other side where the Buccaneers were gathered in an enclosed pool with a bar in the corner and a DJ doing his thing beside the bar, the Big eye was having a difficult time trying to calm the nerves of the blood thirsty deckhands; he wanted them to address the business of the day so that they could leave there on time. He made a promise to them: "Ok, I would like you all to be patient with us the deck masters for a month. Already there are plans. But that is as far as I can go. In a month's time, everything will be settled to your expectations. But for now I need your co-operation if anybody is not ok with that, he can signify." Nobody signified. Although some of the deck masters were having a second thought wondering if the big eye can lead them to the Treasure Island without loosing some of his brothers along the way. "Ok, if that is settled, I would like us to attend to the business of the day. Our lubbers need our attention. Let's go give them the shakes."

The house echoed their response and they left. By the time
they were through with the lubbers it was about 19:30 hrs
and they started about 12:00hrs. Some of the lubbers were
leaping back home, some of them had their tooth shaking;
some would not know what had happened to them until they
sleep and wake up the next day. Well, just so you don't get the
wrong idea, it is just some simple exercises.

Desmond's favourite sweet heart from when he was a
child had been Tracy Chapman. He couldn't understand why
he had this special love for her.

Her voice was so unique: it was like a male and female
voice together. But it was the lyrics of her songs that got him.
Before he gained admission into school, he knew the lyrics
of all her songs off hand and as at that time, Tracy had released four albums. In other words, Desmond could sing all
the tracks in the four albums word for word. This was possible because he had the original albums of Tracy where her
songs are written out. No doubt Tracy is an intellectual and
sometimes it takes intellect to understand her songs. Some
times while day dreaming Desmond wishes to just meet her
in person and have a lengthy chat with her. That was the
extent of his love. In this particular Album *Matters of the
Heart* he was listening to, almost all the tracks were hit tracks
especially *Baby Can I Hold You Tonight* what got his attention more than the rest was the *Bang Bang Bang* track of the
album. On this particular day, he had to put this very track
in repeat mode. He was trying to fathom whom Tracy was
referring to. *Is it the government or some secret societies at each
others throat?* But the more he listened to the track, the more
he came to the conclusion that Tracy must be referring to the

government. The third stanza of the song proved clearly that it must be the government.

All they wanted was to enrich themselves then device a means of making the citizens believe they are working by giving peanuts to small percentage to the citizens to keep them happy and from starting a revolution. But there comes a time when the eyes of the citizens are opened. When they arm themselves to fight whoever is in their way to achieving lasting prosperity and development in their land. A case study of such a situation is the Niger Delta of Nigeria and the Federal Government of the country. Desmond was deep in throught as to how to solve the situation when his phone started ringing. Checking out who the caller was he discovered it was Anita.

"Hi baby what's cooking?" Desmond asked.

"I'm cool baby, your end cool?"

"Yeah, just doing some meditation."

"Didn't figure you as the meditative type."

"Yeah, there comes a time when it is necessary."

Desmond replied

"Hmm, I feel like eating but I'm tired of cooking wondering if you can join me up."

"Why not, since I came back from church, I've been so bored."

"Ok, I'll wait for you to come pick me so we can go together."

"Ok dearie, just give me 20 minutes."

"Don't take too long." she replied then cut the call.

Thirty minutes later, they were strolling hand in hand

into an eatery called *Omega*. It was the kind of romantic sight that makes one jealous. The way they clung to each others and the way they were smiling left no room for doubt that they were in love with each other. Little did Desmond know that Ivie was inside the eatery with her friends. So when they entered, Ivie spotted them but Desmond couldn't see Ivie. Ivie was enraged immediately; but she managed to control herself without letting her friends suspect anything. She was the jealous type. The fried rice and chicken she had been enjoying suddenly became tasteless. Desmond and his girl found an empty spot close to the TV. Which they took. Almost immediately a waiter came to their table and collected their order. Desmond ordered for a plate of jollof rice and moimoi with chicken and a medium size orange juice while Anita ordered a plate of fried rice and salad with chicken and a big size of pineapple juice. While eating Desmond asked, "How is their fried rice today, is it ok?"

"Of course, their rice is always delicious, jollof or fried.

"Really let me have a taste…" Anny heaped her fork and gave it to him in the mouth. Desmond pretended he was not satfied with the taste. He asked for another. She heaped her fork again and gave him. He chewed then shook his head. He said: "Is this what you call delicious?" Desmond asked.

"Of course, didn't you get the taste in your mouth?"

"Ok, let me try it again

"You thief, don't even think of it." she said and they both smiled.

"Ok, what about yours, is it delicious?" she asked.

"Yes of course"

"Lemme have a bite."

"Why, Of course yes."

He used his knife to support his fork so that he could heap his fork with rice. He gave it to her. She chewed then tried to contort her face like she was not pleased with the taste. When Desmond saw her face he asked:

"What, is it not ok?"

"Let me have a taste again." she said. Desmond reduced the quantity and gave it to her. She chewed but still she looked unsatisfied. Desmond didn't bother to ask her; he reduced the quantity by half again and gave it to her but she rejected. She said:

"Hey handsome, what is this? You mean you cannot heap this fork and feed me? Come on, don't be a swine."

"If you think you are gonna add my plate of food to yours unscrupulously, you've got another think coming." They were both smiling. Meanwhile Ivie was at the other corner watching them enviously. Finally their foolishness was over and they left.

Five minutes later, Ivie excused herself, got up and left. It was some minute after 18:00hrs before Desmond came home. He was surprised to find Ivie waiting for him.

"Hi doll, been quite some time now."

"Don't doll me, how dare you cheat on me?"

"What are you talking about?" Desmond asked.

"Don't play smart with me, I saw you and her together."

"You are talking in riddles baby."

"In the restaurant… I was there when you came in. I saw the way you were spoon feeding each other. What's that suppose to mean?" Ivie made herself clearer.

"Now you tell me what that is suppose to mean."

"Don't give me that crap. I saw the way you held her hand while coming in. That sure is proof enough… why deny it?"

"Desmond understood the situation now. Ivie was the type of person that got jealous even when it was obvious one doesn't have anything in common with her. Not only that, she was the bossy type. Desmond had never allowed any girl to control his life, he had no intention of giving any woman the power to do that especially Ivie. He said, "Ok, so what of it. What if she's my new girlfriend huh?"

Ivie didn't bother to start making a scene; he didn't bother to beg like some ladies do. Matter of fact she smiled and said, "You prick, go to hell." But know this, you havn't seen the last of me."

"You are mine and I have no intention of sharing you especially with that bitch you call a girlfriend." She left him standing there like a morun.

Desmond had too much on his mind to start worring about woman trouble. The last thing he wanted was a fight with an ex girlfriend. For Desmond, any woman that excities his interest makes the previous one automatically an ex especially if the former is not humble.

Unknown to Desmond, Ivie was a member of the Daughters of Jezebel Confraternity; a confraternity or a cult whose origin is unknown. They pride themselves of being the most beautiful girls on the campus. For that reason they go out with the most handsome and richest guys on campus. More often than not, they always have an extra boyfriend incase they feel like discarding the one that is less useful to them. That is just for the campus guys. By virtue of their being members of the Daughters of Jezebel, they must be rich. But since most campus guys are struggling to even feed themselves, it was only necessary they get their treasures from older and richer men who come to the campus to patronize them. Although, Desmond was doing financially okay in school, still he cannot afford the expenses needed to take care of a person like Ivie who was a member of the daughters of Jezebel. As a member, if you cannot afford your personal car, then you must look extraordinarily good especially in the dressing. No doubt Ivie was one of the best dressed in her department. Although her family was doing averagely ok, it didn't justify her using expensive Jewelry, clothes and perfumes. If one were to count how many times Ivie has eaten a meal prepared by herself on campus, one would not have to count more than the fingers in one's hands. It was for this reason Desmond distrusted her. Not that he cared. How Ivie manages to pass her exams despite the fact she doesn't read or come to class often baffles Desmond like Adam on Mother's Day. Desmond had never been able to get her around to discuss how she does it. But still on still, who cares.

The Daughters of Jezebel were a notorious group. Most times they get their dirty jobs done through their campus boy friends. This was where campus boyfriends become useful. And when they fail to function as they should, they are quickly discarded as a used pad a woman discards in her period. But there are cases when it becomes necessary to do the dirty jobs themselves especially when it involves murder. On one occasion, a Daughter of Jezebel was having trouble with a lecturerer. It was an old story with the lecturer that he sleeps with his female students and in turn, the female student passes his paper. But with this particular student, the story was the reverse. She failed his paper despite sleeping with him. It had happened twice already and that had wisen her up. She couldn't understand why, *or was it she is extremely good in bed more than his other girlfriends that he decided to keep her?* She thought about it in all directions then she came to a conclusion. Already she was doing the course as an extension student. All her friends had gone for National Service. She was determined to join them. The third time, she met with her friends to discuss the problem. She discussed the situation with her friends and a plan was drawn.

"Hello sir," she was on the phone talking to the lecturer

"Good afternoon."

"Good afternoon Juli. How are you doing?"

"I'm fine sir. Only I'm horny and I need you." The lecturer was already aroused hearing of the word horny.

"Ok sweetheart, are you at home?"

"Yeah I'm at home. Please come quickly."

"Don't worry. Just close your eyes and before you open it, I'm there." she ended the call. True to his word, he was there as quickly as lightning. He said; "Is it that you love my dick so much you cannot get your fill of it?"

"Hey sweetheart, it's been a week now and I've been missing you. Please come to me." The man went to her. She held onto him and dragged him to the bed. They started *smooching* each other. In less than no times their shirts were off. After what looked like 10 minutes the door was opened. This time the lectuerer has put off his pair of trousers and was only in boxers. The man was surprised to find a crowd entering the room.

"What is this? What is this supposed to mean Juli, who

are all these?" Juliet quickly put on her tee shirt and got up from the bed. The man wanted to do the same when a voice from the crowd of girls coming in said;

"Don't even think of it, you bloody son of a bitch. Since you are so sex starved we are going to satisfy your sexual appetite."

"What is that supposed to mean?"

"From now on you do not talk again unless you are asked a question otherwise… well I guess promises are better left unsaid. By the time they were all in the room, seven of them, the man knew better than to be curious.

"Put off your pair of boxers." one of the girls said.

"What?" the lecturer questioned. The girl didn't bother to answer him, from his back, a slap was registered on his face. When he turned to see who, another two was registered on both side of his face. By this time he knew better than to be stubborn. He quickly stripped himself off the pair of boxer. A camera was brought out from one of the bags of the girls. The man's naked body was photographed. With the slap registerd on his face, the man's penis gently recoiled like a shy dog's tail between its legs. One of the girls went to him and started fondling the dick. While that was going on, photographs were taken. It seemed the dick would not respond out of fear. The girl, seeing this knew what next to do. She swallowed his dick and started sucking. In her history of sucking men's dick, only one man's own has failed to respond to the stimulation; she later heard the man was a chronic smoker when she did her research, she discovered that cigarette smoking affects the ability of the penis to erect properly. Some scientists tend to agree that cigarette smoking blocks the pipe or tube responsible for the taking of blood to the penis when it is aroused thereby giving one a weak erection. In less than no time, the man's stock grew. For the lady, it is always a pleasure to see men respond to her job. Of course while this going was going on, photographs were taken showing the man in pleasure. When it was fully erect, the man was tied to the bed and he was raped by the girls. When they were through, the man's phone was collected from his pocket. The wife's number was searched out.

"Mr. Lecturer," one of the girls said but the man was so worn out he didn't have the energy to answer. "You think you are worn out, wait till we resume our second round." The man opened his eyes wide and shook his head side to side "Ok, listen carefully, the same girl continued, "The pictures we've taken so far will be sent to your wife."

"No please, I love my wife so much." the man managed to say

"What do you know about love?" the same girl asked again.

"Please, what is it you want? You don't have to do this. We can work it out."

"Yeah I figured as much. "She turned to Juliet, "Juli baby, this is an extra year for you right?"

"Yeah baby." Juliet replied.

"So far how much do you reckon you've spent?"

"I would say like 50 grand." Juliet replied.

"Come on, don't give us that crap. We know you only too well. There are times when Mr. Bigg's gives you free food because you are their regular customer. The last time we went there together, you spent a minimum of one grand and that was in the evening and I know you must have eaten there in the morning. Ok' let's say you spend two grand every-day at Mr. Bigg's though I know it is more and you've done one month in school because you want to pass this lecturer's course by all means. Now let's do the math to discover how much you've spent on food alone."

One of the girl said, "50 grand," another said, "It's 55 grand" another said; No it is 45 grand, finally one brought out her phone out to do the math. She said "If we are to cal-culate by 30 days, we have 60 grand." The leader of the group continued again;

"Ok, on food alone you've spent 60 grand, what of the school fess? Do extenson students pay the same amount as regular students?"

"Yes." Juliet replied her.

"And the school fees is how much?"

"Ten grand." Juliet replied.

"Ok, that is 70 grand now. What about the transport? I don't know about you but I do know I spend about 50 grand on transport monthly. I'm a good student I go to school ev-eryday even on Sundays. Isn't that right my sisters?"

"Yes." they all echoed.

"Okay, 50 grand plus the 70 will give us how much?" They were racking their brains to tell the answer. One of them said; 'it is 130 grand, another said, "No it is 120". Another confirmed the last figure and said:

"It is 120 grand."

"Ok that is for our sister Juliet. For our troubles, how much do you reckon it is worth?" One of the girls said 30 grand. The leader sparked again.

"Why do you keep insulting this man? He's worth much more than that. I would say 80 G's which if we add to the 120 will give us 200 grand which will be cheap considering his status in this school. Afterall, it is not easy to become a senior lecturer.

"Mr. Lecturer, 200 grand is peanut for you right?" The man was too dumb to say anything.

"I guess that settles it. Tomorrow, we need you to wire the money into this account number. As if by magic a small piece of paper with an account number written on it appeared and it was given to the man. If by 4 pm tomorrow I've not received confirmation alert that it has been paid …. Well, I believe our Mr. Lecturer is a wise man. He need not be told what will happen. Of course it goes without saying that our sister must pass your paper. Rumour has it that she failed again. We want that to remain a rumor and not a fact. Ok? Mr. Lecturer, do we understand each other?"

The man nodded his head. The following day, the leader of the group received a bank alert of 200 grand. The result that has been posted on the board for a week earlier was said to be faulty by the lecturer. It was removed and a week later, another was posted in which Juliet was having an "A" in the man's paper. Finally she was able to go for her National Service.

On another occasion, one of the members was pregnant for a guy on campus when she told him, the guy said it wasn't his business, that she should go look for who was responsible; but the girl was adamant that he was the one responsible for the pregnancy. She kept pestering the guy on what they are to do about the pregnancy. When it got to about a month and the pestering still continued, the guy thought to himself that if he doesn't do something about it now, he's gonna become a father very soon. Becoming a father was the last thing he wanted. As usual she came again. When it was obivious she's determined to give him a baby, he locked the room and beat the hell out of her. Unfortunately, she suffered miscarriage and was taken to a nearby clinic.

Although, she had been doing a great job of hiding it from her friends, when she found herself in the hospital, she knew she must tell them the truth. Finally, they came to see her. "Hey kitten what the heck are you doing in a hospital? Do you want to do breast enlargement?" Her breast was like Rihanna's own. It was so small her friends always tease her that if she gives birth to her baby, her baby might not have breast to hold while sucking.

"No. it is far from it. I'm so sorry beauties. I should have told you long before now. There's this guy I've been crazy about. We've been having unprotected sex for quite some time now though I keep telling him he should use gloves but he keeps insisting that skin to skin is more pleasurable. I was in love with him so I couldn't fight it. Then one day, the unthinkable happened. I got pregnant. When I told him, he said he isn't responsible. All I wanted was for him to tell me whether to abort or keep the baby. But he wouldn't have any of that. Finally when he saw that I will not rest until he gives me an answer, he beat me up as a way of answering and in the process, I miscarried. That is why I'm here."

"Damn!" one of the girls exclaimed, "These campus guys are just good for nothing. That's why I don't date them. They don't know a thing about love, what it means to care for a woman. Now look at what this rascal has done to you. When I tell sisters in the hood not to date campus guys, they think I don't know what I'm saying." She sighed and took a breath.

"This rascal boyfriend of yours, what's his name?"

"Enoma." she answered.

"What department is he?"

"Computer Science."

"Where does he stay?"

"Two streets before mine when coming from the schools gate. His house is the 5th on the left."

"Ok that is all. You just take it easy. Every thing will turn out fine ok? Look what he did to you, almost disfiguring this precious face of yours but then you are a Jezebel, and he can't ruin your beauty. We are terribly sorry for this. We have other things to catch up with. We'll see you again ok? You just manage this meat pie and ice cream. When we come again we'll buy a bigger cup ok? I know you love ice-cream don't you?"

She smiled and nodded her head. The two others hugged and kissed her on the cheek expressing their sympathies before they left. A week later, Enoma was shot dead in front of his house as he was coming from his favourite beer palour around 20:30 hrs. Nobody knew who did it or why it was done. The few of his friends that knew him said he is a nice chap that doesn't have time for cult activities and avoided trouble at all costs. Some others said it was a mistaken identity that got killed instead of the real person that was supposed to be killed.

In the last session before their notoriety made their name infamous all over the campus, making them the most dreaded female fraternity in Uniben, a sweet love story turned sour. Nobody could be sure of it but she said she loved him. It was in their final year in school. They've been seeing each other for close to six months. The guy was from a prominent family in Benin City. He blessed her with many gifts and jewelry; took her to the best restaurants in town. It was a lovely relationship. Soon they started talking of after school: how their life together would look like. Though the guy was careful not to talk about marriage but somehow the hint was given that they could spend the rest of their lives together. There were known all over school as Romeo and Juliet. You hardly see one without finding the other by the side. Out of respect for money, she became loyal. She humbled herself to learn how to cook especially his favourite meal which was *Egusi* soup and pounded yam. Within six months, a transformation occurred that made her sisters in the hood wonder if she was truly in love. In their game, there's no room for love. The transformation they were seeing bothered them. In many instances, they had seen how falling in love has burned their members and so they were always on the look out for their members who fall out of line. They tried to tell her that she's overdoing it; that she should take it easy; that school guys are not to be taken serious but she would not hear any of it. As it is with all fierce love, it became distrustful. Close to their graduation, the guy started to distance himself, giving all kinds of excuses not to see her. He reduced his calls to her. The text messages were also reduced from five to one a day. Soon it become one in three days. This really got her worried. She tried to find out what the problem was, but getting to see him one on one was another problem of its own.

Her friends suggested it could be he was seeing someone else but she said; "Never... I know him, he doesn't like girls. Maybe he's just going through stuff you know?"

"How much do you know him?" one of her friends asked.

"I don't know much but I know this much is true. I was his first love. I was the first person he had sex with. I can tell you, he doesn't like girls and sex." Her friends laughed whole heartedly. One of them said while trying to subdue her laughter, "Who the fuck has been feeding you what? Don't kid yourself baby, finding a guy who doesn't like sex is about as rare as a blond Virgin. They say blond Virgins exist but I've never seen one."

"Why are you guys laughing? What the fuck is so funny about what I just said?" "Ok baby, you take it easy, we are not insinuating anything, just do your homework to be sure ok? Wow! I'm starving who cares to accompany me to Chicken Republic?"

"What do you mean by accompany?" one of the girls asked.

"Is there nothing like *join* in your dictionary? They all got up.

By accompany, I mean you can watch me while I eat."

Don't be a clot; you can afford a bottle of Coke perhaps even a cup of moi-moi."

"If you think I'm gonna piss away my hard earned money I've hustled, you've got another think coming."

"With that kindda attitude, I bet you must be a disappointement to your boyfriends. Life is not all about give me all the the time, you gotta do some giving too."

Don't give me that crap. If anybody is gonna lecture me

on giving, it's sure as hell not you." The one on the offensive said: "I can't believe this shit I'm hearing. A daughter of Jezebel cannot afford three of her friends a cup of ice-cream and moi-moi. This is ridiculus."

"My gosh! from a bottle of Coke to a cup of ice-cream, damn! Ok, I can afford a cup of ice-cream for you guys but never give me that line again that I don't give. I've been taking you out for since God knows when and yet I can count with my fingers the numbers of times you've really taken me out. Meanwhile, the lover girl seemed to have forgotten her broken heart, she was enjoying the drama she was watching. Finally, the one on the offensive said,

"Wow, a cup of ice-cream, you are the best. That's why I love you."

"Go to hell." the one on the defensive said and then resigned to taking them out. And they left the lovergirl behind.

When they were finally gone, the lover girl thought about the whole situation again for the hundredth time.

"Why is my prince charming avoiding me? She thought aloud, she knew some of his friends so she told herself she was gonna start from there on her way back from school the next day. She saw Alfred, a friend of her Prince charming.

"Hi Alfred," way back, she wouldn't have bothered with the pleasantries, she wounld have cut straight into the heart of the matter. But it seemed her prince charming has changed her life in a way she couldn't understand.

"Oh! Hi Ify," she was popularly called Ify though her full name was Ifueko.

"It's been ages since the last time we saw, how do you do?"

She was tempted to say never mind as usual when asked such questions but instead she said "How do you do? When are you gonna be through with your exams?"

"God's grace a week from now." he replied

"Have you defended your project?" she asked again.

"That would be on Friday, the day after my final paper."

"Oh that's good. So after then you can call yourself a graduate."

"Yeah, you can say that again. Going to school is a drag, you woundn't know how happy I am that finally the storm is over. If not that my dad had convinced me that there is something in the loop for me, I woundn't have bothered my-self with school. Has it ever occurred to you that we go to school to learn about people who didn't go school? What pisses me off royal is they set rules or whatever the hell they call it and expect us who went to school to stick by it. What a kingsize drag. My dad kindda hint that I will do my masters programm in Canada once I'm through with my B.sc and if there's anything I want more than anything else is to leave this country for good. No water, no light, poor bad roads, high cost of living. No security, see the way students kill each other, damn it! The country is falling apart."

"I feel your pain brother but we gotta do what we gotta do to survive." in her opinion Alfred can go to hell for all she cares.

In other not to make Alfred suspect anything she asked, "What does your friend think about all these?"

"Which of my friends?"

"Who else do you imagine?" She answered with a question.

"You mean Akenzua your boyfriend?" She looked at him and nodded her head. "Well he's the rich kid, he doesn't careless if the country is turned upside down."

"You mean he's not interested in politics?" She asked.

"Oh, he is indifferent to the subject of politics. You know, it is good to be born into a rich family. You worry less. I can bet my ass, Akenzna has never suffered head ache in his entire life. Have you ever asked him about it?" Alfred asked.

Ify answered cautiously, "The next time he comes I'll ask him."

"Oh, you are not interested in the development of your country too."

"I'm interested in the development of my country but not in politics." she answered.

"Why so? Women are into politics these days and they tend to be doing well?"

"You mean like Patricia?"

"Oh come on, I mean people like Dora and her kind."

"Maybe I'm still young, maybe I don't know a thing about anything but in my opinion any woman who aspires to be a man lacks ambition." She responded. Alfred kept quiet for a while. He pondered what she just said and asked "is your opinion right?"

She nodded her head.

"To tell you the truth I distrust women who are too ambitions." Alfred said. It is alright to be a nurse, home economist, an accountant, Medical doctor and such like things but to think of becoming a governor of a state or president of a country that is going too far. You know, I never thought much about you but with what you just said, I'm beginning to see you in another perspective. Talking about the subject of ambitions: We were discussing it some few days ago. There was this girl in our midst. She's Akenzua's friend. He introduced her as her course mate. We three were discussing the subject but the girl I think Gloria is her name, was of the opinion that women should be given their fair share of human right. She cited many examples of women in administrative role who tend to be doing ok, including the president of Liberia. She's a feminist to the core. She lamented that women are too scared or too reserved to take part in politics. She thinks that if women are given administrative roles in government, the country would be a better place. What do you think?" but Ify was miles away from where she was standing. She was in a world of her own where nobody can reach. Alfred had to ask her the third time before she recollected herself she said "Oh, I'm sorry. I forgot to put off my stove before leaving the house this morning. Look, it's gonna be later things. I gotta bounce."

She left him standing and wondering like a blind lesbian in a fish market. The rest wasn't difficult. She did her homework and discovered that the girl was really in his department.

On the girl's graduation after she had just finished her last paper, she came home jubilating. Bottles of champagne were being popped open as she was coming. A great party had already been planned by her friends. They were cheering and congratulating her. She saw some strange faces but thought they were friends but just about then a strange face brought out a continer from her bag, opened it carefully and poured the content on her saying this is from the Daughters of Jezebel. The content splashed on one side of her face, some on her shoulder and even part of her breast. Immediately she felt a burning sensation on her skin. Her skin began to peel. It was then she realized that acid has been poured on her. Before she could raise her head to see the person who did it, the person was no where to be found. She screamed but her friends were watching. They couldn't do anything. It was later she was rushed to the school's clinic; but by then the damage had already been done. Getting a husband will be the least of her worries. Her face was so disfigured that you begin to think the elephant's scrotum is better looking.

In the streets, the word that kept recurring was *Daughters of Jezebel*. They became the most dreaded female cult on campus.

"So what are we going to do with this prick of a guy that dares to tell me it is over?" Ivie had summoned her crew to her house. After they had discussed the issue she asked her crew the question. One of them said "This is what we are going to do."

"Alora Sealords," Desmond was addressing his fellow deck masters.

"Alora me rugged big eye." they responded. Desmond continued, "So what of our brother that was bloodied?"

From all indications, he's gonna make it. But he's pretty bad, the steerer answered. Desmond nodded his head.

"What about our Maphite brothers? What are their re-actions? They must be itching to strike again. Now that it is obvious our brother is gonna make it."

The steerer answered again. "So far no attempt has been

made on any Lord. But that's not to say we shouldn't watch our back. It is just some few weeks to exams. They may want to surprise us then. "Me K. what do you think?" Desmond asked.

"They know better than to strike again but I'm not saying we should underestimate them. From our past dealings they know what will happen but let's be on guard."

"What about our black and blue friends."

"They don't see us to be people to be scared of. They have reduced their guard." The KMS answered.

"Good, that is what I want. Now is the time to hit. We'll take the 3 frats unaware. When they least expect it. Two weeks time we make the HIT."

Chapter 10

Prior to the two weeks before they were to make HIT, their charity work was carried out by the Deckmasters. The SJ went from faculty to faculty giving faculty heads a covered waste bin. On the waste bin was written 'courtesy Ban' and when asked by the faculty head or the secretary what is the meaning of BAN, one of the Lords will gladly reply, "Brothers Across Nigeria" in some cases, pictures were taken to freeze the event so that it will last forever. Of course waste bins were also dropped in the Vice Chancellor's office. The charitable work did not go unnoticed. Three days later the VC on behalf of the schools ruling council, thanked the Brothers Accros Nigeria for the charitable work they have done. The note of thanks was posted on the noticed board of the school for all to see. Once again the other confraternities were green with envy. Two weeks later happened to coincide with the 3rd jaw jaw/initiation of lubbers into the Brothers across Nigeria. By this time almost all the students had finished their exams except for the medical students who had a different school calender from the rest of the school. But as it is with life, unforseen events despite all the preperations will always pop up. The unforseen event they didn't see was war. Some few days to the end of the exams, the birdboys struck a blow to the Axemen. Reason was that the previous semester, one of their members was disrespected by an Axeman in a drinking bar. When the birdboy who was the victim tried to retaliate, other Axemen on the scene pounced on him. The birdboy sustained some wounds but it was not serious. It happened after the first semester when everybody had gone home for the break. The birdboys couldn't retaliate because the school was empty. They decided to hold their grudge till the second semester.

The deckmasters quickly gathered for an emergency meeting.

"Alora me big eye what are we to do, should we wait till their war subsides?"

"No, it is perfect for us. It'll reduce the stress of fighting the three fraternities; afterall we are not supermen to be fighting three fraternities together. This is what we are gonna do."

For security reasons, the hotel they've been using for their JJ's was changed. They booked a hotel that was newly built in the interiors of the government residential area. The area was still developing. The houses around were scanty. The roads around the area were still untarred, though a construction company was already in place to start the project. The lubbers, 25 in number were navigated to the hotel by a bus. Other Lords were to navigate themselves to the hotel on their own. They got to the hotel by 19:00hrs. For security reasons they decided to do the initiation over night. The Big eye and his 1st shipmate were the only deck masters present with the lubbers. Others would join them in time. The Big eye approached the receptionist who showed them where they are to use. Getting there the big eye ordered the lubbers to change into the traditional regalia for induction.

Around 20:00hrs, the Axemen decided to hold an emergency meeting to discuss recent event about what really happened, why it happened and how to strike back at the birdboys. That same time, the birdboys decided to meet to discusss strategy. From experience they knew the Axemen will surely strike back. They decided to use the no. 3 man's hostel at B.D.P.A. Uniben for safety reasons because the hostel was fenced. The excos were the first to arrive. They decided to move in twos. The *Ibaka* that is their no.1 and his second in command were the 1st to arrive. Just as they got to the gate of the hostel they heard a gunshot but couldn't tell from where but that was the last thing they heard. They fell on the ground. To make sure they are dead, the people responsible for the shooting came to the gate to see. But they didn't bother to check if they are alive, they fired another shot to their heads and left. The others hearing of the gunshot, ran for their lives. 10 minutes in a secure location, they called their big eye to give him the signal. The big eye listened, nodded his head and asked them to come to the anchor point. He ended the call and called the second group. He gave them their instruction and ended the call. The Axemen were holding their meeting behind their chief's house. Behind the house was a small farm which they hold their meetings. Some 30 minutes into the meeting, one of them received a call. It was the no. 3 man of the house, the chief butcher. He said: "Yeah, who be this?"

"We just drop two birdboys now for B.D.P.A. *una still dey the meeting?*"

"Yeah we still dey but we go soon move .Identify yourself.

The line went dead. He passed the message to the rest of the house. There was some kind of Jubilation in the house. In the Black Axe movement, it is alright to carry out personal vendetta. But the house must be informed so that everybody can be on guard. 80% of the Axemen are so headstrong they cannot be controlled. And so it was natural to find squads pulling their own HIT without the order of their chief. So when a call like this came in, they didn't bother to be worried. It was one of those things that happens every now and then. Ten minutes later, a car pulled up to a stop close to where the meeting of the Axemen was being held. Three young guys alighted. Navigated their way to where the meeting is being held. As they were coming, some Axemen were already echoing the clarion call "Aye Axemen, Aye Axemen!" the three young guys coming had no choice but to echo the response with disgust. It was dark so the Axemen couldn't see the three young guys properly. But they saw the black beret the young guys were flying. That was enough for them. As they got near, the chief and his chief butcher came forward to congratulate them on their heroic act but just as they got near, an English barrel was pointed at them. Before they could understand the situation a shot was fired at them. The two of them dropped down instantly and died. Another three from the crowd were hit by flying bullet. The three fell but were not dead. Others hearing of the shot, took to their heels. The three guys didn't bother to waste their bullets on the three other Axemen that fell. Afterall they are not barbarians but fine boys who are well cultured. They went to the chief and his chief butcher, they fired another shot to their heads to confirm them and they left. Their car had already been reversed and was facing the exit direction waiting for them. As soon as they were in, the car sped off. Ten munites later when they were at a secure location, they called their big eye. The BE listened, nodded his head and asked them to come to the anchor point. It happened at Ekosodi, the village of the Axemen. He called the third group and gave them their instruction.

That very same day happened to be the graduation party of one of the Maphite's top ranking officers. Because it was a graduation party, civilians were allowed to come. Close to the hostel were the party was being held a grey *Audi 80* was parked some few block away: it was some few minutes after 21:00hrs when they got the call from their big eye. Immediately they stepped out of the car and went to the venue of the party. The venue was located at Omoruyi Street off Uwasota Road. The house was at a disadvantage. The south side of the house was fenced as well as the east and west side but the north side was opened making it impossible for anybody to run sideways or backward. There were little gatherings outside of different groups. It was easy to tell which groups are the soldiers and which groups are the civilians. When the Buccaneers entered the compound they scanned the people present and discovered that the general and some of his officers were standing close to the street the compound was facing. Maybe because it was a party or maybe it was the beer they've been drinking, they didn't bother to be observant as military men. When the three Buccaneers got to where they were standing, one of them looked but he was a little tipsy so he didn't give them a serious observation. He turned his head away as soon as he saw them. One of the Buccaneers brought out a short English barrel from inside his leather jacket he was wearing. He pointed it at the General. At that same instant, the guy that saw them coming that was a little tipsy decide to see what they are up to since he cannot hear their voice despite they are close by. But it was too late. As he turned he heard a shot. He fell instantly to the ground. The general fell too. Two others felt buninig sensation in their arms but they ran for their lives first. Later they'll have to see what really happened. The Buccaneers went to the general and the other guy that fell, shot them in the head again and ran with the crowd that was running helter-skelter. They got to their car which was already positioned in the exit positioned. As soon as they climbed in, the car sped off. Later they made a call to their BE. He nodded and ask them to come to the anchor point.

By 22:00hrs, all the rolling squads were at the hotel for the induction ceremony of their lubbers. The BE was at the entrance of the hotel to welcome them. A red mercedez 190 rolled in followed by the gray Audi 80 and followed by the white Toyota Haice bus that was used to convey lubbers to the hotel. As they stepped out, the BE embraced them and clawed them the traditional way. They were ushered into the hotel into the place reserved for them. Some deckhands were already drinking from the traditional brew meant for only buccaneers. As soon as the rolling squad enterd, a cup of brew was given them each. The BE ordered the deckhands and his fellow deckmasters to converge. When they converged, he said; "Alora Sealords!"

"Alora me rugged big eye!" the house echoed.

"As some of you must have observed, some of our deck-masters havn't been around but now they are back. It is not something we glory in but when it becomes necessary then we have no choice. Why they havn't been around was because they were attending to business. As of now all our accounts have been setteld. The Axemen, Eiye or Birdboys or what-ever the hell they call themselves, and the Maphites were all hit this evening."

"*Chiakwu, Awoskelebe, ehn ehn, crook kuroo coo.*" the deck-hands were making different funny sounds like witches in a coven at the mention of victory. One of them echoed, "Big eye, you are too too rugged." the Big eye was not a person of many words. He concluded by saying, "We've all agreed that even if the tides are high and the sea is rough," the house joined him to echo the last phrase "the treasure must be found."

He continued, "Now that this is settled, let's get to the business of the day." The house echoed their response and went to where the lubbers are. Some were already sweating like a chilled bottle of beer brought out from the fridge. The lubbers were filed into a single row and were moved to a swampy area of the hotel. While the JJ/initiation was go-ing on, seasongs were being sung by the Buccaneers. The traditional brew was passed around. Some were smoking their cigararettes. Marijuana is strictly prohibited in the Buccaneer's ship so there was nobody smoking it. In the end, only 22 lubbers were inducted. The other three were sacri-fised. Next year if they are lucky they would be inducted, that is if they still choose to be in the train. But most times, they always come back because thy have seen the light. By 05:00hrs the folloing day, all the inductions were completed. The BE ordered all to converge so that he could address the newly initiated lords and give them some orientation. When they were gathered the BE said; "Alora SeaLords!"

"Alora me rugged big eye!" the house echoed. The Big eye continued "For our newly inied brothers, I want to tell you that you've made the right choice to become lords. This confraternity started sailing since 1972. Since then the confraternity has undergone so many changes in order to weather the storms threatening it. I'm proud to tell you that this confraternity-Brothers across Nigeria a.k.a Buccaneers association Nigeria, can be found in every state of our country, Nigeria. There are frigates and galleons all across the country. You may be wondering what the hell is galleon and frigates, but as you continue to sail with your brothers you'll come to discover that Ban is more or less an intellectual society or a way of life for traditional Buccaneers. Traditionally, our mode of communication is not written down. You get to know these things as you sail with your brothers. Trust me, they'll be glad to enlighten you. We are sailors more or less like unscrupulous adventurers. So in the course of sailing, you communicate with your brothers as a sailor. That's why it is in your interest to sail with your brothers so as to get orientation, as an unscrupulous adventurer. What makes you rugged is your orientation. You must be intelligent. Buccaneering is wide it is important you keep reminding yourself: *what is this and why is that*. You may not have known what you've done today but as you continue to sail. You will discover the beauty of this noble confraternity and what it stands for and the meaning of what you've done now. Time will not permit me now I would've loved to orientate you more. It is almost day break. Hmm, ok, next Saturday is our ST (shiptail) when you come, we'll give you more oriention. It's almost 06:00hrs, I would like you to wash up and change into the clothes you wore to this place after then you can leave. Once again welcome on board."

The house echoed their response and dispersed.

The Axemen were confused as to who had really hit them: was it the Bird Boys? But from all indications, it didn't look like it was them. Another thing again, as a fact, the BirdBoys were also hit. Who pulled the HIT on the Birdboys? Is it some headstrong Aye, was he shot while coming to tell us at our shrine? If shot, who shot him but more importantly where is the body if shot. Or is it just one hell of a trick to get at us by the birdboys, but then again we've known these people only too well, they cannot pull off such a job. They haven't got the balls to pull such stunt. Or is it the Bucaneers, but their minds were so paralysed, by the shock of it all that they couldn't think straight anymore. At the same time, the birdies were thinking the same thing and coming to the same conclusion: "Is it the Buccaneers?" The loss of their 'ibaka' was too much for them. They will have to forgo vengenance for now and think about who will lead them; for it is important that they find themselves a leader. And moreover, the session has ended. On the other hand, the Maphite knew who had hit them but the loss of their general was too much for them. They will have to wait till next session, before thinking of vengeance or not. They have to mourn their loss and find somebody to lead them. Only the Axemen attemted to hit but it was a mistaken identity. The lubber in question was rolling with the Buccaneers 24/7. He was bloodied mercilessly by akites he couldn't survive it. He died instantly. It ended at that but who will blame the Axemen in times of war, nobody is completely innocent but such is life that one cannot be too careful. Even if he is not rolling with the Buccaneers, death would have found another reason to take his life.

On Saturday the following week, the Buccaneers converged again for their ST. A bus was hired to convey girls to the venue. After about three trips, the ratio of girls to guys was 2:1. By 12:00hrs, the DJ was already doing his thing. In another corner of the hotel, some lords were gathered singing seasongs. They were in a circular form gyrating. In the dance hall, the girls were taking their seats trying to fill their eyes with the splendour of the hall. Almost immediately, crates of different alcoholic drinks were passed around. Some took and some rejected. For those who rejected, non alcoholic drinks were given them. With the drinks in their hand, they became relaxed.

The D J was doing his thing. By 13:00hrs, all the newly inied lords were present keeping some of the girls company while some others went to join the group that were gyrating. By 14:00hrs, the big eye and all his pieces were present. They flirted with the girls for a while then the big eye ordered all the newly inied lords to assemble at the back of the hotel. When they were all gathered, the BE said to them. "I believe by now you've gotten some orientation so I'm not going to bother about those little things. I'll just give you the basics, the general things you are supposed to know about our confraternity," He paused to light a cigarette while some old Lords were coming around to add anything the BE may be forgetting. But only temporary, the business of the day demanded they should rock the beauties in the dance hall. They were not about to let that go to waste. The BE, done with the lighting of his king size London cigarette, drew on it greedily. Then exhaled. The deckhands were watching and waiting. He continued. "First of all, what the hell is confraternity?" the deckhands were looking at one another. He continued; "It is unfortunate that the word these days has a negative notion. People have come to believe that the word is synonymous with evil. But that notion is wrong. But if I may ask, what do you think is confraternity?"

One of the deckhands said; "Secret cult", another said; "Secret society."

"You see, that is wrong. I cannot believe that with all the JJs you've gone through you still think of confraternity as a secret cult or a secret society. Ok, the first thing you have to know about confraternity is that it was gotten from the word fraternity and fraternity was gotten from the word 'fraternus' a Latin word. And the meaning of the word simply put is brotherhood. Brotherhood is an association or community of people with a common interest, religion or trade so what does that tell you? One of the deckhands instead of answering asked: "Does that mean that the church can be called a confraternity?"

"Yeah, you are right. The church can also be called confraternity. Confraternity, which is also from a Latin word means the *coming together of people of the same interest*. Matter of fact, God instituted confraternity when He created man. Don't know, but it seems He was fucking bored and he wanted to fraternise and so as God, He did the sensible thing; He created man. What is more again, Adam was becoming a nuisance with himself, he wanted somebody to fraternise with. God saw this and pitied him. He knew how it sucks to be alone. He did another good thing again, He created a woman for Adam. So simply put, confraternity is the coming together of brothers of the same interest. So if you are calling BAN a secret cult or secret society, it is an insult to this noble fraternity. If you had been a month old in the game, I would have had you hauled by my hauler. In any case BAN is a confraternity and not a secret cult."

"So what is the difference between a fraternity and a cult?" One of the deckhands asked.

"I was coming to that but I want you to understand this properly. Wole Sokyinka was bold enough to want to sue the Federal Government because the FG dares to call them secret cult. Not that he would have won but what I want you to understand is your right as a lord. A policeman cannot come here to arrest any of us because we are a registered fraternity. We are different from the rest. We are unique in our own fashion. So while others may be violent causing terror and panic in campuses, we ain't cut out for that shit. You must be well behaved and disciplined at all times. Matter of fact, staying out of trouble will be your business. As for the question; *what is the difference between cult and confraternity?* Well, there is a thin line that separates the two. Just like the word confraternity, cult in itself is not evil. It depends on the purpose or intention of the gathering. Although while cult may be a little eccentric, confraternity is easily understood. In the Catholic Church for instance, there are various confraternities. We have confraternity of the Most Holy Rosary, Confraternity of the Miraculous Infant Jesus, Confraternity of Christian Mothers. There are so many in the Catholic Church. The church understands it to be a small religious group. But in the secular world, it is seen as evil by most but this is not true. A confraternity, aside being open to all must carry out charitable act, every now and then. At least to make others aware of what they stand for. I dunno if any of you saw the new waste bins in all the faculties. If you look carefully, you will see the words 'Courtesy: Ban' written on it. Some of the deckhands nodded their heads that they saw it. One of them said: "I was really impressed by the charitable act. From then on, I knew I was into something great." The Big eye smiled then continued; "By the time you salt to sail in the high seas, you'll see more of these things. Back to what I was saying, while a confraternity is seen as a brotherhood to help the society they are in, a cult is seen as something occultic in the secular world. But then again, this is not true. The word cult was gotten from the Latin word "cultus" meaning worship. In the spiritual or religious world, cult refers to a system of religious devotion directed towards a particular figure or object. In the Catholic Church again, we have such things like cult of the Virgin Mary and Cult of the saints. I believe some of us here who are not catholics, must have accused the Catholic Church of worshipping the Blessed Virgin Mary. Although some in the Catholic Church will call it honour in order not to confuse their protestant brothers. There are different kinds of worship. There's one that is reserved for

God alone. It is called 'LATRIA'; this one that demands we love God with our whole hearts and being. There's another kind of worship that is less than the one we give God but which is due the angels and Saints of God. That one is called DULIA". These are Latin words which were gotten from Greek words. You can find them in the dictionary. But since the Blessed Virgin Mary is the queen of angels and saints, a special worship or reverence is accorded her which is called HYPER-DULIA. The word "HYPER" was gotten from the Greek word "HUPER" which means above, over or beyond. In other words, the reverence or worship accorded the Blessed Virgin is higher than that of the angels and saints but less than the worship reserved for God. So the Catholic Church worshipping the BVM and angles and saints of God in not doing anything contrary to the Bible. I am so sorry I had to digress a little. It is just that confraternity, cult and the church are closely related, so that you cannot talk about one without talking about the other. As for the difference between a confraternity and a cult, the main difference is that while one is not strictly religious but can be religious; the other is strictly religious. Now that is the reason BAN cannot be called a cult but a confraternity because we are not a religious order but we believe in God and carry out works of mercy or charitable acts. As a lord, it is important to know the creed. The creed of this confraternity is: *we shall not discriminate against any tribe, religion or race be it of this nation or another and in the course of doing so... so may our blood clot within our veins.*

At that moment his phone rang. He excused himself and answered the call. The call was from Ivie.

"Hi love, what is this, just a little quarrel and you re-fused to call me. Such nonsense, I thought you're smarter than this."

The innocent attack paralysed him. He fell in lov again. He said; "Oh hon, I'm terribly sorry; I've been going through a lot. It's nice of you to call and I'm glad to hear your voice. Have you travelled now, the school is almost empty."

"Dessy you are becoming so dumb. You mean you are not going to ask me about my exams?" immediately Desmond felt sheepish.

"Ok, ok, ok, how did your exams go?" he asked.

"Are you asking me? Desmond became confused. Instinct told him to end the call but the sound of her voice still thrilled him. Although this was the part of her he misses nonetheless it was also the part he distrusts. To him Ivie was like dyna-mite, one has to be careful. He gave up trying to figure her out. He asked her defeatedly, "What the fuck do you want?" she detected defeat in his voice and thought to herself, *I can handle this prick anytime.* "Didn't you enjoy those times we had to gether?" she asked.

Desmond wondered briefly where the conversation was heading. He said;

"Mmm, Mmm, so what of it?"

"Come on, don't be a prick, don't you have some sense of appreciation, I love you no matter what you may think. I cooked this great meal. I figured we should have one last great time together before I leave for Lagos. Moreover I've not had sex since the last time we fought. I'm horny."

Just like a TV put on by a remote control, Desmond felt energetic immediately at the hearing of sex. He was touched by her sense of appreciation. He was smiling when he said, "Didn't know you have much brain. I din't see you as the cooking type. So you can cook afterall?"

"I guess there's more to me than meets the eyes. Meanwhile where the fuck are you anyway? I'm at your house."

"Wait, *wait, wait,* you are not in my house right now, are you?"

"You bet your sorry ass I am." She replied.

"Hey, I'm in the middle of something, do you think you can come to this new hotel at Ugbor, it's called Heaven's Ville Hotel."

"What the fuck are you doing in a hotel, are you in the hotel with that sorry ass of a bitch you call girlfriend? If you think I'm in for a threesome, you've got another think coming. I'm at the house waiting for you."

Desmond sighed. He wanted to tell her he was done with this shit but he found himself saying, "Ok I'll be there shortly." Then he ended the call.

Some of the deckhands were already smoking their third cigarette. By the time he was finished with his call, he sighed. "I'm sorry, where are we again?" "Difference between confraternity and cult". One of the deckhands said.

"Ok I remember now, like I said before, the main difference between a confraternity and a cult is that a confraternity does not necessarily have to be a religious order but can be while a cult is strictly a religious group. But when a cult is for the intention of worshipping any weird being or object, other than God and His angels and saints, then that cult becomes occultic. I guess we all know the meaning of occult. As for secret cult, that's about it. Secret cult is just secret cult.

It's against the constitution of our country Nigeria as well as most countries in the world if not all. So that is about it when it comes to confraternity, cult, secret cult and occult. If you have any question please feel free to ask." But the newly inied Lords were itching to go grab some asses in the dance hall. The question was as good to them as light to a blind man. But still one of them asked, "Do we have frigates in other parts of the world?"

"Yeah we do have. We have in the seven continents of the world. Rumour has it that SBC is contemplating changing the name from Brothers across Nigeria to brothers across nations." The BE looked at his watch then said, "It's some minutes after 16:00 hrs, I guess we have to join our rugged brothers in the dance hall. From what I hear, the girls are tempting to touch especially with the provocative dance they are dancing. Let's do ourselves some good. He decided to have some fun before going to meet Ivie at his house. He danced for another two hours drinking two bottles of beer in the process. Since it was a hotel it was easy for Lords to navigate their temporary girlfriends to unbooked rooms in the hotel. By 19:00 hrs, more than half of the Lords were no where to be found.

Desmond was already in his house but to his disappointment, Ivie has gone. He saw a big flask on his reading table. He thought briefly that he must change the position of where he keeps his key. That must have been the food she was talking of he thought. He opened it and discovered that the spiced spagetti with a nice aroma was still hot. Immediately he felt hungry. He went into the kitchen to get himself a spoon.

By 20:00 hrs, the DMs were through with their romp. There was still one last thing to do before next session. Now that the BE had graduated, he needed to anchor the big eye ship to an undergraduate. He had asked about their opinion and they had said they would think about it. It was time for the DMs to leave; they wanted to have one last word with the deckhands before they attend to business.

"Alora me brothers, on behalf of the the big eye and his pieces, I echo rugeedly for you all. I don't have much to say except that you all should pipe low and be observant. The big eye is not around now, he needs to attend to some other business. Anyway you are all aware that there is still RS, so I guess you don't need to be told to submarine. I can see some of you are itching to leave; well, you can leave. SO me rugged brothers."

"SO me rugged steerer." The deckhands echoed and dispersed. The steerer turned to his fellow deckmasters, "I guess we can attend to our business." They went to a secluded place.

"Alora DMs, most of us will be travelling next month, but before we travel we need to know who the next big eye will be. Although the big eye doesn't need us before he choses who to suceed him; nonetheless he needs our opinion. So among us who do you think is rugged enough to eye the deck?" the FF said, "Anderson" the hauler said 'Greham', the KMS said: "Instead of discussing it among ourselves, why not go to him so that we can put forward our opinion and hear his own." The steerer nodded his head and said, ok. The 1st shipmate said: "Do we have to go to him this night, moreover he is with his girlfriend, I say we should go to him tomorrow. This idea of going to him this night is dangerous."

The issue was deliberated for 10 minutes whether to go his house or not but finally they decided to go. Getting to his house, they knocked but they didn't get any answer. They used the buccaneering code to knock, yet no answer. The SJ said, "I guess he is on the 3rd round. The steerer knocked again for the seventh time yet no response from the inside. The KMS didn't like it at all. His thinking was that they were an easy prey for their enemies. Worse was that the compound wasn't fenced. Out of annoyance he said; "Let's burst open this door, we can always get it fixed." He was about to match open the door with all the force he had when the 2nd shipmate said, "Alora, everything is not by force, lets try turning the door knob before you do what you are about to do. The KMS turned the knob and much to his surprice, the door opened. Lying on the floor was Desmond. Foam was coming out of his mouth. At first they thought he was drunk and vomitting but at another glance they discovered he was not moving, that was when they rushed inside. The 1st shipmate grabbed him, raised him up, felt his purse then bent over him to check if he was breathing, he raised himself up and said to the rest, "He is dead."

Chapter 11

A handful of luck, they say, is worth more than ten truckload of wisdom. Luckily for Desmond, the 2nd shipmate was carrying with him a black stone. That precious stone you can find only in Jerusalem. When the 1st shipmate pronounced the big eye dead, the 2nd said: "No that cannot be." To him Desmond was one of the most careful people he had known except when it comes to women and on that he had told him to be careful. That they can be dangerous spiritualy and physically. But Desmond had said: *women are more or less like toys they make you happy just as toys make children happy.* The 2nd shipmate didn't fight it, he just said, 'be careful.' He had come to believe that in life nothing is what it is. An event thought him that lesson. A close friend of his who was an Axeman went out with his friends to have some fun. In the process they drank some bottles of beer. They really had a good time. In the evening the friends dropped him in his house. Some 20 minutes later, his friend died of poison. On a certain day when he was travelling to the Eastern part of the country, in the bus a man got up and started preaching about the miraculous black stone and the world of good it can do for anyone using it. Among the goodies about the stone was how it can drain any poisonous substance from the body. He was fascinated. He decided to buy and give it a trial. Since then he has been carrying it along incase of emergency. So when it was confirmed that his big eye ate poison, he decided to try his miraculous black stone. He cut a part of his big eye's body and placed the stone there. Surprisingly, just like a magnet, the stone stuck to the part of his body that was oozing blood. They all stayed with him that night. It was around 03:00am that the stone dropped after sucking the poison off his blood. Thirty minutes later Desmond opened his eyes, his rugged brothers were shocked. They never believed for a moment that it would work. The following morning they took him to a deckhand's house to care for him properly.

The following week, the DMs were all assembled in a bar to iron out the last issue. The big eye cleared his throat: "I want to thank you all for your support. But for you all I would have been dead." The DMs were quiet. Some of them were dragging on their cigarette greedily like there was no tomorrow while others were sipping from their beer. The big eye continued: "While I was half way down the grave, did any of HLs tried to retaliate?" The steerer shook his head and said "No."

"Ok then, I have called us here to discuss the way forward for this noble fraternity. It's about the issue of anchoring. I have decided to anchor to Greham. My reasons are many but some of them are intelligence, smartness, familiarity with the waters and most importantly boldness and courage. Does any of you have any reason why he shouldn't be the big eye of this deck?" He looked at them one after the other as they all shook their heads. Only the KMS said if he had had the chance to choose, he would have chosen the same person the big eye hadchosen. The big eye said: "It is settled then. Tomorrow we'll do the anchoring and invite some Lords to witness it."

"At where?" asked the KMS.

"Hmm, I guess Heaven's Ville Hotel is okay. Is that okay by you all?" They all nodded their heads. I guess that is that then." The BE said. The KMS had something troubling him so he said: "This bitch of yours that tried to poison you-what are we gonna do about it? Our policy still remains *no price no pay*"

The Big eye went into his shell for a while and thought about it all, if not for his fellow deckmasters, he would have been dead by a poison from a girl. After much thought, he said unconciously: "Women are necessary evils." the KMS said I can dig her out in a matter of days. On hearing I can dig her out, the big eye crawled out of his shell. He said; "Let her go. We are not some kind of *mafioso or* organised criminals. We are good patriots of our country and we should leave it at that." With this, the KMS was relieved though he didn't know why. Their bottles of beer were empty and two parkets of London menthol cigarette was dead. They wanted to leave because the coast wasn't that clear despite that students were no longer on campus. Anybody can take anybody unaware. The big eye, knowing this said, "That will be all." He got up, clawed each of them and bade them to sail on. They all replied him in the same fashion and bade him to 'sail on!'

EPILOUGE

The exact death toll of confraternity- related murders is unclear. One estimate in 2002 was that 250 people had been killed in campus cult -related murders in the previous decade. However, these figures are of insignificance when compared with recent confraternity activities in Benin City, Edo state capital in 2008 and 2009 with over 40 cult related deaths recorded monthly. It is unfortunate that the goal for which most of these confraternities were formed is being deviated from. The Pyrates Confraternity, the first to sail the waters of Nigeria universities is a role model for the rest including the Buccaneers. Although, the Buccaneers, to a large extent have tried in their own right. But more effort is needed. Thank goodness that the cry to stop deck activities had deen heeded by most decks.Before long, others will follow suit. For the rest fraternities, they need to trace their origin and see what they stand for. Many a dispute can be resolved without bloodshed and violence. They need not live up to the name TERRORIST as a certain paper termed them.

The Eiye Confraternity for instance, which originated from the University of Ibadan in 1963 started as a secret society known as the Eiye Group but later metamorphosized into Supreme Eiye Confraternity (SEC). The confraternity was esterblished to make positive impact on the social-political mind, social cultural, physical and mental development of its member and was indifferent from other conventional confraternities. But it is sad to note that they and the Axemen are like cats and rats, always at each others' throats in Benin City. And the Black Axe Confraternity or moverment which was established in 1976, by seven young men, was formed for the motive of building a body to fight against the oppression against the Black race. Rumour has it that it was established in South Africa to fight against the Apartheid war when the whites were trying to dominate blacks in their own continent. Blacks had no choice but to fight since the oppression was too much. That can be understood. But in Nigeria, there's no basis for fighting since there are no whites trying to oppress us. If they can focus their energy in trying to fight the ills of society and the ills of government, they would be doing a great job.

One way the government can assist in reducing gang violence in the universities is by getting these confraternities to register themselves in whatever institution they choose to operate in. Their activities should be drafted out; names of member should also be documented. If any crime or violence should be associated with any of them, then the appropriate punishment should be meted out to that individual or if possible to the members of that confraternity which the individual is affiliated to. Take for instance, the Junior Chambers International, Rotaract and Rotary club; these are social organization established to impart leadership skill in their members. They have their code of conduct which members are to adhere to religiously. And if they fail in carrying out their obligation of living up to their name in the society, a punishment is meted out to the erring member. With such a code of conduct guiding the members, it is difficult for a member to deviate from that code and do something so stupid as to warrant disciplinary action against him or the members of his fraternity by the school authority or the government of the country. Social organizations like the JCI, Rotary and Rotaract club are more or less like a confraternity and they have been known to produce great leaders. Who says the future president of our country cannot come from the Pyrates Confraternity or the Neo-Black movement of African or the Maphite's or Vikings Confraternity? All we need to do is stand aside, look into ourselves, and find those resources we were blessed with by God and channel it to the development of our country. When this can be done, there is no telling the height of greatness we will achieve.

CPSIA information can be obtained
at www.ICGtesting.com
Printed in the USA
LVOW11s2350020418
572082LV00001B/55/P